Ron gets inside the mind of a teenager better than anyone I know. Students will be able to identify with the characters and be moved from complacency to action as they come to grips with the reality of eternity.

Rob Paugh Senior Youth Pastor
Grove City Church of the Nazarene

River's Edge is a compelling story of God's continual presence and compassion. Set in a small Ohio town, the story of an unlikely hero unfolds in the midst of everyday life and often tragic circumstances. It's a hilarious and sobering look at what happens when ordinary lives are infiltrated by extraordinary courage and unconditional love. For those who enjoy a story with loveable characters and a positive message, this one does not disappoint. Allow yourself time to sit down and relax with this book because you won't be able to put it down.

Dr. Nyle Sexton
Associate Pastor
Rocklane Christian Church

RIVERS**EDGE**

RIVERS**EDGE**

a novel by Ronald McCarty

Tate Publishing & Enterprises

Published by Tate Publishing & Enterprises, LLC
127 E. Trade Center Terrace | Mustang, Oklahoma 73064 USA
1.888.361.9473 | www.tatepublishing.com

Tate Publishing is committed to excellence in the publishing industry. The company reflects the philosophy established by the founders, based on Psalm 68:11,
"The Lord gave the word and great was the company of those who published it."

Book design copyright © 2009 by Tate Publishing, LLC. All rights reserved.
Cover design by Melanie Harr-Hughes
Interior design by Stephanie Woloszyn

Published in the United States of America

ISBN: 978-1-60799-178-6
1. Fiction / Christian / General
08.12.30

CHAPTER 1

"Dear diary: Today we will set a record for the hottest day ever in May. I'm glad, too, since Michael Fredricks, who by the way is only the cutest guy in school, asked me to go waterskiing with him. He's six foot two and has brown curly hair and the greenest eyes you have ever seen. He's a linebacker on the football team and works out all the time. Need I say more? Anyway, I've been dying to go out with him, and he finally asked me. I'm so nervous. I think I'm about the luckiest girl in school. I've got to go now. Michael will be here any minute."

Kelly closed her diary and walked over to the mirror above her dresser. She studied her five-foot-eight-inch frame, looking for any blemish that might show in her bathing suit. She wondered if the jean shorts she was wearing were too faded. She turned and checked until she was certain that she looked just right. Putting her hair on top of her head, she pulled it back, twisting and turning it until it looked worse than ever. Finally, in desperation, she took out her brush, combed her long blonde hair back, and placed it into a ponytail. When she finished her hair, she stared intently at her image in the mirror.

"No way! I look horrible! It's the jeans. They're too faded." Kelly ran to her dresser and began to rummage through the drawers as if there were a prize waiting at the bottom.

Michael pulled the car over to the side of the road. He could see Kelly's house from where he was parked. His hands were sweating, and his mouth was dry. He began to think he had made a mistake. *What's wrong with me?* he thought. *It's not like I haven't dated other girls. Why should this one be any different?* Michael could feel his heart beating against his ribs. *What if I say something stupid? Or forget to do some of those things girls expect a guy to do? Like open a car door, or tell her how pretty she looks.* Michael adjusted the car mirror and made certain that his hair was in place. He readjusted his mirror and grabbed the shift lever. *I may as well get this over with.*

Putting the car in gear, he drove the remaining half block to her home and pulled into the driveway. He shut off the engine, took a deep breath, opened the car door, and walked what seemed to be at least a mile to Kelly's front door. Hand trembling, he rang the doorbell.

"Kelly! I think it's that hunk you've been waiting for." Kelly's mom smiled as she thought about a time when she was just as nervous as Kelly was, waiting for a boy. Of course, as it turned out, she'd had good reason to be nervous. The boy was now her husband.

Kelly panicked as she heard the doorbell ring. She had one leg on of the fourth pair of shorts she had tried on. "Stall him! I'll be down in a minute." Kelly looked at herself in the mirror for what seemed to be the one-hundredth time. Then panicked. "Mom! Have you seen my bathing suit?"

Connie Carlisle smiled. "I've already packed it along with your towel. It's down here in the living room. Which, by the way, is where you should be."

Connie walked over to the door, opened it, and greeted a very nervous young man. "Hi! You must be Michael." Connie stuck out her hand. "I'm Connie Carlisle. Come on in."

Michael wasn't used to shaking hands with a woman. He was always afraid of hurting them. Much to his surprise, Connie Carlisle greeted him with a handshake worthy of most men. "Nice to meet you, ma'am."

Connie smiled at the stiffness of his greeting. "Please don't call me 'ma'am.' It makes me sound like an old woman. I know to someone your age I may seem old, but thank goodness I'm not." Connie walked over to the couch and asked Michael to join her.

Michael felt as if his legs weighed a ton as he walked the few feet to the couch. He sat down and tried to find a comfortable position, first folding and then unfolding his hands, then crossing and uncrossing his legs. Connie couldn't help herself as she began to laugh.

"Michael, please relax. I'm very harmless. My husband, on the other hand, is a karate teacher who weighs two hundred and fifty pounds." She enjoyed the panic that etched Michael's face. "I'm just kidding, Michael. My husband is only about five ten and weighs about one seventy-five. Believe me, the only thing he knows about any kind of karate is the kind that comes in a bottle."

Michael's look told her that he had never heard of Hai Karate cologne before. "It's a cologne, Michael. Please just feel free to be yourself. I promise not to bite."

Michael slowly began to smile. "I'm sorry, but for some reason I'm very nervous."

"No problem. So is my daughter. I only hope you two can relax enough to get to know each other."

"Me too!" Michael began to relax and felt his breathing begin to return to normal. "You have a really nice house, Mrs. Carlisle."

"You sound like you're talking to the old maid down the street. My name is Connie. If you're not comfortable with that, then you can leave."

Michael was startled at first, and then he saw the smile light up her face. "I'm sorry. I guess I've never met a mom who was as nice as you. Except my mom, of course."

"I consider myself to be in good company. Thank you for the compliment. Now, as you kids would say, *chill*."

Kelly heard Michael and her mom talking. She hoped she wasn't boring Michael with…"Oh my gosh! She wouldn't! Not the family album!" Kelly quickly finished getting ready and bounded down the stairs, almost falling on the last few steps.

Kelly's mom looked up and smiled. "That's my girl. Always ready to make a grand entrance."

Kelly was obviously embarrassed by her actions but tried to cover it up. "You know me, Mom, I always want to be the center of attention." Kelly regained her composure and smiled at Michael. "Hi, Michael! You look nice."

Michael stood up. "Me too."

Kelly and her mom looked at each other and then at Michael. In unison they smiled and asked, "What did you say?"

Michael's face turned bright red as he tried to recover from a very dumb statement. "I meant to say that you looked nice too. I guess it didn't come out too well, did it?"

Kelly and her mom began to laugh. Soon Michael was caught up in the laughter and began to feel a lot better. He was starting to be glad that he didn't chicken out. He had never realized how beautiful Kelly was until he saw her laughing. She just seemed to light up the room with her laughter.

Kelly wiped the tears from her eyes. "I guess we'd better be going before we both embarrass ourselves again. My mom will never let me forget my graceful entrance."

Michael shook his head in agreement. "I'm sure I've made a lasting impression."

Kelly's mom looked at Michael and smiled. "All I can say, Michael, is that you will fit right in with the rest of us."

Kelly grabbed her beach bag and purse and kissed her mom. "I'll see you later, troublemaker."

Connie tried to act insulted. "Of all the nerve! Michael, can you believe what my daughter just called me?"

"Cool it, Mom! He's not going to fall for your sympathy act." Kelly walked over to Michael, took his hand, and said, "Let's get out of here before she really gets carried away."

As Kelly and Michael walked toward the door, Connie

stood up. "Michael! Please make sure she holds onto the rope if she tries to ski. After all, she is a blonde."

Kelly grabbed a pillow from a recliner and threw it at her mom as she ran toward the door. "Come on. Let's get out of here."

Michael and Kelly made it through the front door just as the pillow hit the wall. As they ran toward the car, Michael looked at Kelly. "Do you and your mom act like this all the time?"

Kelly stopped, looked back at the house, and smiled lovingly. "Yeah! We really do. She's like my very best friend."

Michael opened the door for Kelly. He didn't want to blow another chance for a good impression. He closed her door, walked to the driver's side, and slid into the seat next to Kelly. As he was fastening his seat belt, Kelly asked him a question. "How about you?"

Michael looked puzzled. "How about me what?"

"Do you get along with your mom?"

Michael sat back against the seat. "We've gotten a lot closer since my dad died."

"Do you miss your dad?" Michael looked at Kelly and then focused his eyes straight ahead. Kelly wasn't certain, but she thought she saw a tear begin to form in his eye.

He sat silently for a moment, his lip quivering slightly as he answered. "Every day. He was my best friend. We did everything together. We hunted, fished, rode bikes together. He taught me how to play sports. I guess that's one reason I still play. I know that he would be proud of me. He always was."

Kelly could see the love in Michael's eyes. She hoped she hadn't asked something that she shouldn't have. "I'm sorry. I hope you didn't mind my asking."

He looked at Kelly and smiled. "I never mind talking about my dad." Michael turned the key in the ignition, started the car, and pulled away from the curb. Kelly watched him as he maneuvered his car onto the highway. She felt a closeness to him that she had never felt for a boy before. Silently, she thought, *Yes, I'm sure I'm the luckiest girl at Riverton High School.*

CHAPTER 2

Lake Jackson, located in a valley surrounded by the gentle rolling hills of Stark County, was a flurry of activity. On any given day the lake was crowded, but after a long cold winter, a day like this brought people out in droves. The sound of powerboats filled the warm air like the sound of giant angry bees. Picnic areas were full. Children were laughing and running, chasing each other as if they had just been let out of solitary confinement. Parents were trying to find a place to relax where the children wouldn't run over them.

Michael pulled into the parking lot of the marina just as Jeff Peterson, one of Michael's close friends, pulled in. Jeff parked his car and ran over to greet Michael and Kelly. He opened the door for Kelly. Michael kidded him, "That's it, Jeff, make me look bad in front of Kelly. That's supposed to be my job."

Jeff helped Kelly out of the car. "Don't pay any attention to him. He's just jealous of my good looks."

Michael smiled, for he knew full well that Jeff was embarrassed because he was overweight. He was five foot six in shoes and weighed two hundred thirty-five pounds.

Once, Michael had told him that his ruddy complexion and red hair made him look like a fat Ronald McDonald. Michael loved to tease him, but Jeff would always have a quick comeback. In spite of their lack of common interest, the two boys had become very good friends.

Michael walked around the car and gave Jeff a playful shove. Jeff feigned pain and said to Kelly. "That's just like these jocks. They can't compete in looks so they rely on their animal nature."

Kelly joined in on the fun. "Now, boys, you don't have to fight over me. I don't want to have to choose."

Michael shoved Jeff again. "Now see what you've done? She's starting to act like you."

The trio was busy talking when Brad Lewis walked up. He had been the star linebacker before Michael had come along and acquired the position. Brad took every opportunity he could to try to make Michael look bad. At six two, two hundred twenty pounds, he may have intimidated some people, but his efforts were lost on Michael.

"Fancy meeting you here." The sarcasm in his voice was evident to everyone, including Kelly.

"What are you doing here, Brad?" Michael didn't want to embarrass Kelly, so he didn't say what he would like to say.

"Jeremy is my cousin. He invited me to go skiing with him."

Michael felt the anger building up inside him. "Jeremy never said anything to me about you coming."

Brad's smirk made Michael even more angry. "Small world, isn't it, Michael? See you at the boat." Brad turned and walked away from the group.

Michael watched him leave and then turned to Jeff. "Just what I didn't need. I can't believe Jeremy invited him. He knows how Brad feels about me."

Jeff tried to comfort him. "He's a jerk. Just ignore him."

Kelly spoke up. "We don't have to stay, Michael. We can go somewhere else."

Michael knew that she meant well, but the last thing he was going to do was let Brad make him look bad in front of Kelly. "It's no big deal, Kelly. Like Jeff said, he's just a big jerk. Come on. We'd better get to the boat before he tells Jeremy we're not coming." Michael locked his car, and the trio headed for the dock.

Jeremy was busy getting the boat ready when Michael, Kelly, and Jeff walked up. Michael playfully grabbed Jeremy, who jumped up like he had been shot. He grabbed Michael, and the two began to wrestle. Jeremy managed to put Michael in a headlock. But Michael, being several inches taller and outweighing him by about twenty pounds, quickly regained the advantage. Jeff looked over at Kelly, who didn't quite know what to think.

"Don't worry. It's just two jocks trying to outdo each other."

The boys finished their match and began to laugh while trying to regain normal breathing. Jeremy smacked Michael playfully. "Don't scare me like that. Especially in front of Kelly. She may think I'm a wimp."

Kelly smiled. "Don't worry, Jeremy; I already know that you are."

Jeff and Michael responded with a joint, "Oooh."

Michael loved it. "Way to go, Kelly! She's got your number, Mr. Quarterback."

Jeremy feigned anger as he moved toward Kelly. "You're mine, lady. How dare you make fun of a star."

Michael jumped in front of Kelly. "No way. She's with me. You'll have to go through me first."

Jeremy laughed and grabbed Michael. "Have it your way, lover boy."

The two boys were on the ground when Kelly looked at Jeff. "Do they act like this all the time?"

"Pretty much."

"What a couple of jerks. Making fools of themselves in public."

Michael recognized Brad's voice and felt the anger start. The two boys stopped what they were doing and stood to face Brad. Jeremy knew the situation between Brad and Michael, so he spoke first in order to try to avoid a confrontation. "Brad, if you're going with us I suggest that you try to act like you have some brains."

"Why did you ask me to come if you don't like the way I act?"

"First of all, you invited yourself. I don't mind, but we came out here to have a good time, and I don't want you to cause any trouble."

"Me? Why does everyone think that I'm the bad guy here? I just don't like guys who think they're cool when I know they're not."

Michael started to say something when Kelly spoke. "Hey, could we just stop all of this and get out on the water? If you all keep letting your macho images get in the way, we'll never get anything done."

Michael knew that Kelly was right, but he hated to let Brad get the last dig. He started to say something but thought better of it when he saw Kelly watching him. "Kelly's right. Let's get off this dock and do some skiing."

Jeremy finished loading all of the equipment and motioned for everyone to get on. He asked Michael to unhook the boat from the dock and push them off. The water was choppy from all of the boats on the lake. Jeremy guided the boat skillfully through the maze of boats as they headed for the ski area. The ride was quiet, each one locked into his own personal thoughts. Michael noticed that Brad was watching Kelly. He started to say something to him but knew that it would only embarrass Kelly. *Still,* he thought, *it would be kind of nice to have an excuse to throw him overboard.*

Jeremy pulled the boat to a stop once he reached the ski zone. He stopped the engine and looked at his friends. "Who wants to be the first one to go?"

Jeff laughed. "Could you find a better way to put that? It sounds kind of final. 'Who wants to be the first to go?'"

"Is that a yes, Mr. Wizard?"

Jeff swallowed hard. He was well aware of the fact that he was no athlete, but he didn't want to be a chicken either. "Sure, I'll be the first."

Jeremy handed Jeff the life vest and waited until he finished putting it on. "Ready?"

Jeff looked at him and tried to manage a smile of confidence, but only managed a nervous grin. "I guess so. This vest is going to hold me up, isn't it?"

Jeremy smiled. "Don't worry, Jeff, they tested it on an elephant."

"Cute, Jeremy. Real cute."

Michael tried to encourage him. "Come on, Jeff, you'll do great. It's like riding a bike. Once you learn, you never forget."

"Have you ever seen me on a bike? Besides, this is only the second time I've tried this, and I don't want to talk about the first."

Reluctantly, Jeff slid into the water. The moment he hit the water, he was sorry he had volunteered, for the water was ice cold. He let out a yelp and wanted desperately to get back in the boat. "Man, this water is cold."

"Don't be a wimp. If you can't take it, let someone go who can."

Michael started to lash out at Brad, but Jeremy beat him to it. "Brad, don't start. You know the water hasn't had time to warm up yet. You may yell more than he did."

"I doubt that very seriously."

Jeremy threw the towrope to Jeff. "Take hold of the handle, and I'll play out the rope." Jeremy started the engine and carefully guided the boat forward, asking Michael to keep an eye on Jeff. The rope tightened to a point where it began to lift Jeff out of the water, and

Jeremy knew that he was ready. He looked back at Jeff. "Are you ready?"

The cold water was getting to him, but Jeff managed to nod. Jeremy moved the throttle to the full position, and Jeff felt the rope pull hard. He tried to remember all of the things he had been taught the first time he had been skiing, but all he seemed to do was make a huge wake. The strain got to his arms, and the rope shot out of his hands. He bobbed in the water like a huge buoy while Jeremy maneuvered the boat back into position. Again and again Jeff tried to get up on top of the water only to lose his grip. Finally he signaled Jeremy that he had suffered enough. Jeremy pulled the boat next to Jeff and stopped the engine. "Give up, big guy?"

Jeff was too weak to answer. He took off the skis and handed them to Michael. He reached up like a little kid who just wanted someone to rescue him. Michael struggled to lift him into the boat. "Man, Jeff, you've got to lose some weight. I need a crane to get you in."

Jeff was too tired to joke. He just sat and shivered as he removed the cold, wet vest and handed it to Jeremy. Jeremy held up the vest and smiled. "Next?"

Brad grabbed the vest and began to put it on. He saw an opportunity to show off, and he grabbed it. He finished putting the vest on, stood up and plunged into the water.

The cold water took his breath, but he was determined to show his toughness, so he remained silent. "Throw me the rope!"

Michael looked at Jeremy. "Like he doesn't think that water's cold. Right!"

Jeremy nodded in agreement. "He'll never admit it. Go ahead and throw him the rope. He can't wait to show off."

Michael looked at Jeremy and frowned. "Don't tell me he's good at this."

Jeremy shook his head in affirmation. "Unfortunately, yes!"

Michael felt his heart sink. He threw the rope to Brad and sat down. *That's all I need,* he thought. *Just my luck, he had to come along.*

Jeremy guided the boat into position, and Brad yelled for him to go. He was out of the water like a shot. Michael watched in horror as Brad skillfully maneuvered back and forth across the wakes. He put the rope between his legs and let go. Then he lifted one foot and shot across the wake and came up almost next to the boat. Michael looked at Kelly, who was intently watching, and wondered what she was thinking. Brad skied for what seemed like hours to Michael and then signaled Jeremy that he was letting go.

Jeremy swung the boat back around to pick him up. When they reached him, he was smiling from ear to ear. "Let's see you top that, Mr. Superstar." Brad got back into the boat and handed the vest to Michael.

When Michael put the cold vest on, it gave him goose bumps. He hoped no one would notice, especially Kelly. He stood up, looked at Kelly, and plunged overboard. Hitting the water was like hitting a tub of ice after a warm shower. He managed to subdue any comment, knowing that Brad would love it. He regained his composure and asked for the towrope. Brad threw the rope to him and smiled a sinister grin. "Do you know how to ski, or do you want some expert advice?"

Jeremy looked at Brad. "Don't push it!"

Michael ignored his comment and signaled that he was ready. Jeremy tightened the rope and shoved the throttle forward. Michael shot to the surface with ease, and was soon moving back and forth behind the boat like a pro. He felt his confidence begin to return and began to try to show off without being too obvious.

The lake was narrow at this point, so Jeremy swung close to shore to give Michael plenty of room to make a turn. As Jeremy began the turn, Michael shot to the outside of the boat in order to gain speed. He squatted low to the water and held the rope with one hand. He was watching Kelly, hoping that she was watching him. It was for that reason that he did not see a stump sticking just above the surface of the water. His skis caught the stump and Michael was whipped completely around, tossing his body hard against the surface of the water. Michael tried to orient himself in the water. He could hear the boat coming and Kelly screaming. His vision was blurred, and he began to feel his body going numb. He wasn't certain if it was the effect of the cold water or something else. He could faintly hear Kelly's voice as his world went black.

CHAPTER 3

"Michael! Michael! Come on, honey, it's time to get up."

Michael rolled over, looked at the clock, and covered his head. "Six o'clock? Man, it's way too early to get up." He rolled over on his side and tried to reposition himself.

"Michael! Don't make me have to come in there. I know you are trying to go back to sleep, but don't try it. You don't want to be late for your first day of school."

"Yes I do!" he mumbled.

"I heard that, Michael."

Michael rolled over. "No way. She couldn't hear me. I could barely hear it myself, and I said it."

"Yes, I could, and I heard that, too."

Michael looked at his bedroom door, and there stood his mom. Arms folded and just the hint of a smile mixed with a little frustration. "So that's how you did it? You sneaked into my room."

"You never know where I might be. Just remember that. Now get out of that bed before I have to throw you out." Mary turned and walked back toward the kitchen.

Michael threw the covers off and sat on the edge of the bed. He stretched, looked at the clock, and fell back on the bed. Thoughts of his dad filled his mind as he began to recall the painful events of the past year. He thought of the way his dad had suffered in his struggle with cancer. He remembered the pain and the hallucinations from all of the medication. *Why did you have to die? Why did you leave mom and me like this? Now I have to start my senior year at a new school.*

Michael knew that his dad had not chosen to die and felt a little guilty for his thoughts. But he was dreading this day more than any he could remember. He was popular at his old school; all of his friends were still there. *It's not fair!* he thought. *It's just not fair.*

Michael heard his mom in the kitchen and knew that at any minute she would be yelling again, so he reluctantly got out of bed. He walked to his dresser and looked at himself in the mirror. He was busy surveying himself when he happened to see the picture of his hero taped to the wall beside his dresser. Dick Butkus! Known as the meanest man in football.

Although Michael was not around when he had played, he had seen films of him, and he was definitely his kind of ball player. Michael looked at the poster, then at his own reflection in the mirror. He tried to look as menacing as Dick Butkus. After a few appropriate growls, Michael turned to go into the bathroom and fell over his gym bag.

Michael's mom heard the terrible crash and rushed to see if he was all right. She came into the room just as he was picking himself off of the floor. "Are you alright?"

Michael, red faced, assured her that he was. "I was just trying to imitate Dick Butkus."

"Who?"

Michael pointed at the picture taped to the wall. "He was the greatest linebacker of all time. At least that's what dad said."

Mary smiled, for she knew that if his dad had made that statement, Michael would have believed it. She knew how close the two had been. "I thought for certain you had hurt yourself. Now please quit fooling around and get into the kitchen for breakfast."

Michael smiled as he looked at the picture of Dick Butkus again. "I'll bet you weren't as clumsy as I am." Then he walked into the bathroom to finish getting ready.

When Michael entered the kitchen the smell of bacon and eggs stirred a hunger that he hadn't been aware of until that moment. He walked up behind his mom and grabbed a piece of bacon from the plate on the stove. She smacked his hand and reminded him of his manners.

"Nothing to eat until it's all ready. Now sit down at the table like a gentleman."

Michael loved it when his mom tried to make him mind. Sometimes she treated him like a little kid, but he knew she meant well. He took his place at the table and took a drink of the milk she had placed there. "I'm going to ride my bike to school."

Mary turned to face him, visibly disappointed. "I thought I was going to drive you to school."

Michael laughed. "I don't think so, Mom! It's going

to be hard enough starting a new school, let alone having your mom drive you there."

"If I didn't need the car, you could take it, but I have to work today."

"It's okay, Mom. It's not that far to school. Besides, I need the exercise."

Mary finished placing the food on the table and sat down. She paused as she watched Michael fill his plate. She knew how hard it was going to be for him and felt more than a little guilty for putting him in this situation. But she felt certain that she had made the right decision. "Michael, I'm sorry that we had to make this move. I know this past year has been very hard on you. I wish I could make it all go away, but I can't."

Michael saw the tears fill the corners of his mom's eyes and knew that she was struggling for the right words. "Mom, I know what you're trying to say, and it's okay. We both left a lot behind us, and I know you're hurting just as much as I am."

"I just couldn't stand all of the memories in that house or in that town. It was just too painful. I could see your dad everywhere I went."

Michael wanted to assure his mom that everything would be alright, but in his heart he didn't feel that way. He was angry and hurt, but he loved his mom too much to tell her the truth about how he felt. He reached out and placed his hand on his mom's hand. "Mom, I love you, and I understand why you had to leave. I'll be fine."

Mary looked into Michael's eyes. She could see his father in those eyes. He always tried to assure her that everything would be alright regardless of the situation, even when he wasn't certain himself. Michael smiled at his mom, picked up his fork, and began to finish his breakfast. Mary sat in silence, her mind filled with thoughts of what may lie ahead for them.

— — — — — — — —

Riverton High School was a flurry of activity. The first day of school brought the usual traffic jams both inside and outside the school. The building itself was beginning to show the wear of its fifty-two years of use. What once was a sparkling clean building was now a building in need of serious repair. One more sign of a struggling rural economy.

The buses were busy emptying their cargo of young people who were wishing they were any place but there.

Michael pulled his bicycle to a stop just down the road from the school. He watched the activity with a great deal of apprehension. *Why do I have to face this?* he thought. *I can't help it my dad died. It's just not fair. Mom could have made the adjustment. We didn't have to leave.* Michael caught himself, and realized how selfish his thoughts were.

Maybe this will work out for the best. Sure. I mean, it can't be all bad—can it? He stood for another few moments and then pushed off on his bike to finish the last few yards to school.

Michael walked through the big weathered doors and into the hallway.

"Hey, new kid!"

Michael stopped, turned, and saw a short, stocky boy with red hair moving toward him. He stopped in front of Michael and stuck out his hand.

"Hi! My name's Jeff! Jeff Peterson."

"I'm Michael Fredricks."

"I know who you are. You're that football star we've heard so much about." Michael smiled, "Star? I don't think so."

"Don't be so modest. Everyone knows that Coach Bryant can't wait to get you on the team."

"I hope he won't be too disappointed. Stockdale was a small-town school."

"Like this is a giant city?"

"No, but we may have used a different kind of game plan than you use here."

Jeff said, "First of all, I don't know a game plan from a house plan. Most importantly, I'm not a jock. I know you may have mistaken this bulk for muscle, but believe me, it's just bulk. So I have no idea how they play here. I do know they take football very seriously in this town."

"Just the same, I hope I can fit in here."

"You certainly fit the mold with those muscles and no neck." Ordinarily Michael might have been offended by his remark. But there was something different about Jeff; for some reason he felt drawn to him. "There is one person who may not be too happy about you playing here."

"Who's that?" Michael asked.

"Brad Lewis. He is, or was, the starting linebacker for our team. He's been putting you down all summer."

"He doesn't even know me."

"He doesn't need to. All he knows is that his position as starter may be in trouble."

Great, Michael thought, *just what I need—something else to deal with.*

Jeff could sense Michael's uneasiness. "Hey, don't worry about him. He's just a real big jerk. Besides, someone needs to take him down to size."

"I'm just here to finish my last year of school and play some football. It's up to the coaches who plays where."

Jeff wisely changed the subject. "Do you know where your first class is?"

"Not really."

"What is your first class?"

Michael took out a crumpled piece of paper and unfolded it. "History with Mr. Fuller."

"You'll like him. He's not only the history teacher; he's also an assistant coach. Come on! I'll show you where your class is."

When Michael walked into the history classroom, he felt as though time had stopped. Every eye was on him, and he felt that no one liked what they saw. His thoughts were interrupted by a strong voice coming from the front of the classroom.

"Mr. Fredricks, I presume."

Michael looked up and saw a tall, well-groomed black man moving toward him. Although he had some gray in his hair and beard, Michael thought he looked very young. He held out his hand and greeted Michael with a grip every bit as strong as his own. "I'm Mr. Fuller. You must be Michael."

Michael felt as though there was something very special about this man. "Yes, sir."

"Come on in and take a seat."

Michael moved to the only available seat in the classroom. Unknown to Michael, this seat just happened to be right next to Brad Lewis, the young man Jeff had said was so upset by the threat Michael posed to his position on the football team. Jeff smiled, wondering if Michael realized that he was about to take a seat right next to the young man who was so upset by Michael's presence?

"Could I have your attention up front now?" Mr. Fuller knew all too well that the curiosity surrounding Michael's arrival held the attention of the entire class. "We need to get started. I would like all of you to fill out this attendance roster. I'll need your name, address, and phone number. Please write legibly, or print the information."

Michael's mind began to wander, and soon Mr. Fuller's voice was replaced by his own thoughts. He looked around the room and tried to imagine what everyone was like. Would they like him? He wanted so much to fit in but knew only too well how often new kids were shunned. How should he act? Should he play it cool or be the first one to break the ice? He didn't like being placed in this position. Before he knew it, the bell sounded signaling the end of the shortened period.

"Class dismissed! Mr. Fredricks, could I see you for a moment please?"

Michael got up from his seat and walked toward the front of the classroom.

"I just wanted to give you an official welcome. I think you'll like it here. The students for the most part are good kids."

"If there's anything you need, just let me know."

"Thank you, Mr. Fuller."

"Coach! You might as well get used to calling me coach. Everyone else does."

Michael smiled. "Yes, sir, Coach."

"Don't be late for practice. You do know where the football team practices, don't you?"

"Yes, sir. I rode my bike past there last night."

"Good! You best be on your way. If you're late for your next class, they might just give you a detention."

Michael smiled, said goodbye, and walked out into the busy hallway.

The warmth he felt with Mr. Fuller was a sharp contrast to the activity of several hundred students trying to find their way to their rooms. He looked down the hallway, took a deep breath, and moved off to his next class.

The day passed quickly, and as Michael walked toward the door that led outside, he reflected on the events of the day. All in all, it wasn't as bad as he thought it would be. He was really impressed with Mr. Fuller, and a lot of the kids had come up to introduce themselves. Maybe it really wouldn't be as bad as he thought it would be.

"Hey, Michael! Wait for me."

Michael turned and saw Jeff running toward him. "Whew—I guess I'm in worse shape than I thought."

"You do look like you just ran a couple of miles."

As Jeff struggled to catch his breath he managed to squeak out, "Actually it was more like a hundred yards, but I'm working on it."

"What's next? Two hundred yards?"

"No, actually I'm going to run over to the D.Q."

"The D.Q.?"

"Yeah, you know, the Dairy Queen."

Michael laughed. "That's just what you need."

"Got to keep up my image, you know. You headed to the football field?"

"Sure. You going to try out?"

"For what? Water boy? I don't think so. I just thought I'd walk over with you. I want to see the look on Brad Lewis's face when he sees you."

"He may not even care anymore."

"Believe me, he will definitely care."

The two boys walked toward the football field. One with his mind fixed on getting into the groove of practicing. The other anxiously hoping to see someone that he perceived as a braggart put in his place.

As Michael and Jeff approached the practice field they saw a group of players standing at one end. As they drew closer, one young man yelled, "Hey! Here comes the superstar."

Michael looked at Jeff. "Let me guess. This must be Brad Lewis."

"In the flesh."

Michael just continued to walk toward the locker room.

"Hey! I'm talking to you, Superstar. You too good to talk to the little people?"

Michael stopped.

"Don't pay any attention to him, Michael. He's just a jerk," Jeff cautioned.

Michael looked at Jeff. "I guess you're right. It's just a big waste of time."

Brad and the others began to walk toward Michael until they blocked his path. "I don't think he heard me, guys. Or maybe he's just afraid to talk to us."

Michael's jaw began to twitch as he grew angrier. He stood toe to toe with Brad. He felt the weight of all the pain and frustration he had been dealing with stirring up inside him. He knew that if he let himself, he could lose complete control.

"How about it, Superstar? Don't you like us?"

"What do you think, Jeff? Should I talk to this clown, or just ignore him and hope he's smart enough to take the hint?"

Ordinarily Jeff would not let himself be put in this position, but he was feeling pretty safe with Michael there.

"He's never been known as a smart person, so he may not know when to leave."

Brad snapped at Jeff. "You'd better watch your mouth, geek, or I'll shut it for you."

"You're right, Jeff. He doesn't know when to leave."

Brad reached out to grab Michael, but was stopped short when someone grabbed him from behind. It was Coach Bryant, the head football coach, who had walked up to the group unnoticed. "That's quite enough, Mr. Lewis!"

"He started it, Coach!"

"I doubt that very seriously, Brad. It's no secret that you've been putting him down all summer."

"But, Coach—"

"But nothing. I want you and your group of cronies to give me two laps. Maybe it will help settle you down for practice. We can't get anything done with an attitude like yours. Now go!"

If looks could kill, Michael and Jeff would have been dead. "I'll talk to you later," Brad snarled.

"Make that three laps, Mr. Lewis."

Michael watched as Brad and the others ran off and he heard Jeff breathe a sigh of relief. Coach Bryant looked at Jeff. "Unless you have decided to join the team, Jeff, I would like to talk to Michael alone."

"No sir! I think I've had all the excitement I can stand for one day. Besides, I think they have a triple fudge royal sundae with my name on it at the Dairy Queen. See you later, Michael."

"Okay, Jeff. Don't eat too much."

"What, and spoil this physique?"

Michael smiled as he watched Jeff waddle off the field.

"Sorry about Brad's attitude, son. I'm afraid we may have some problems with him unless he can control his temper."

Michael turned to face his new coach. He had liked

him since the first day he'd met him. "No problem, sir. I just want to play football. I'm not worried about him."

"I'm sure you're not. But I'll keep an eye on him just the same. He's a good player, but he's a hothead and very intimidated by your presence."

"He's never seen me play. Why would he be worried?"

"He's watched some of your game films. So he definitely has seen you play."

"I just hope I can play as good as everyone seems to think I can."

"I know talent, son, and you definitely have talent."

"I'll do my best, Coach."

"I'm certain you will. Now get on over to the locker room and get some gear. We'll never know if you can play unless you get started."

━ ━ ━ ━ ━ ━ ━ ━

Michael felt exhausted as he rode home after his first practice. Coach Bryant really knew what he was doing. Michael felt good about playing for him. He noticed during practice that Coach Bryant walked with a limp and wondered if it was an old football injury. He wanted to ask him but knew the coach might not want to talk about it. Maybe someday he would feel comfortable enough to ask him.

Michael noticed a group of young people sitting outside of a drugstore. He was particularly interested in the girl with the long blonde hair. He was so intent on the group that he didn't pay attention to where he was going.

"Hey! Watch where you're going!"

Michael stopped his bike and looked at the young man driving a small red sports car. He was smiling, and Michael recognized him as Jeremy Wethers, the quarterback for the team.

"I'm sorry—I was just deep in thought."

"Kelly Carlisle."

"What?"

"Her name is Kelly Carlisle."

"Whose name is Kelly Carlisle?"

"As if you didn't know. I saw the group you were watching. She is the only one in that group who could hold someone's attention like that."

"Do you know her?"

"Sure! She's in my youth group at church."

"Is she some religious freak?"

"Kelly? Not really. She seems to enjoy the group and gets pretty involved, but she's still pretty cool."

"How about you?"

"How about me what?"

"Are you religious?"

Jeremy laughed. "I don't think so. I go because my parents make me go. It's okay, but I just don't get into it."

"Does she date anyone?"

"Just me."

"I'm sorry. I didn't know."

Jeremy began to laugh so hard he almost fell out of

his car. "I'm just kidding. I just wanted to see the look on your face, and it was sure worth it."

"Very funny."

"Come to our youth service with me sometime. I'll introduce you."

Michael knew by the look on Jeremy's face that he was just joking with him.

"Hey, are you up to a ride in a convertible?"

"I'm on my bike."

"No problem. I've got a bike rack on the back. Come on! I'll show you all the exciting spots in town. Should only take about ten minutes."

"Are you ever serious?"

"No way! Life's too short."

It didn't take Michael long to make up his mind. "I've always wanted to ride in one of these things anyway."

"Things? Is that any way to talk about a prime M.G.B.?"

"Sorry. Lost my head."

The boys fastened down the bike, climbed into the car, and pulled away from the curb. As they drove past the group of young people, Jeremy yelled at the top of his lungs, "Hey, Kelly! This guy here likes you." The group turned to see one young man trying desperately to crawl under the dashboard of a small car, as the other one laughed with gusto.

CHAPTER 4

The next few weeks passed quickly and uneventfully for Michael. He fit into the football program just the way Coach Bryant felt he would and very quickly established himself as the key to the Riverton defense. The frustration of the move was being softened by the new friends Michael was making. The only thing that bothered him was the fact that he had not met Kelly, the girl he had seen at the drugstore on his first day of school. Jeremy had offered to introduce him, but Michael was not too sure just what Jeremy would do. Michael had learned quickly that Jeremy was seldom serious.

■ ■ ■ ■ ■ ■ ■

Kelly Carlisle was a typical young lady of seventeen. She enjoyed school and being active in her church youth group. She wasn't certain what she wanted to do with her life, but the one thing she did know for sure was that she wanted to spend it with someone very special. She was planning to go to college but was not positive about her major. She had considered teaching or social work but was trying to be open to what God wanted her to do.

She just felt certain that He had a very specific plan for her life.

Kelly was busy trying to stuff twenty pounds of books in a bag designed to hold ten. As usual, she was running late, and she knew that her mom was waiting to take her to school.

"Kelly! It's getting late, dear. You'd best get moving."

"I'm almost ready, Mom! I'll be down in just a minute." Kelly hated mornings. She said she never understood why they had to come so early. She was sure God had never intended for life to be that way. She was pushing the last book into the bag when the seam on the side of the bag split. "Oh no! I don't believe this!" Kelly grabbed the bag, said a silent prayer, asking God to hold it together until she could get a new one and ran out of the bedroom.

As Connie Carlisle was pulling out of the driveway, she looked over at Kelly and noticed that the side of her book bag was split. "Kelly, what in the world happened to your bag?"

Kelly looked at the bag and smiled at her mom. "I don't know. I didn't realize that anything was wrong."

Connie laughed, knowing full well what she had done. "You've been trying to put too many books into that bag again, haven't you?"

"Well, they should be stronger than they are. How am I supposed to carry all of my books? I'd need a bag the size of a large suitcase."

"How many bags have I bought you over the past few years? I must have interest in the company by now."

Connie shook her head and smiled. "I guess those blonde roots go deeper than I thought they did."

"Very funny, Mom."

"Your dad wanted me to ask you if you wanted to go bowling with him Friday night."

"I'm going to the game with some of my friends."

"You seem to have taken a sudden interest in football games, Kelly. There wouldn't be any special reason for that would there?"

Kelly looked at her mom and smiled. She felt her face flush a little but tried to act innocent. "Of course not, Mom. I just happen to like football."

"That was sure a sudden change. I thought you considered it too barbaric?"

Kelly knew that her mom could see right through her. "Well, maybe there is a new reason for going."

Connie laughed, "What's his name?"

Kelly lay back against the seat and sighed. "His name is Michael, Michael Fredricks. He's new at school this year, and he's an absolute dream."

"Let me guess. He just happens to be a football player." The look in Kelly's eyes told Connie all she needed to know.

"He's not just a football player. He's the best one on the team, and he's drop-dead gorgeous."

Connie laughed. "That's a term I've never heard before. Sounds like you've got a bad case of infatuation."

"I've never met him, Mom, but there's something special about him. Jeremy knows him and promised to introduce me to him."

Connie shook her head and laughed. "Your dad is not going to like losing his little girl to another man."

"Get serious, Mom. I haven't even met him yet."

Connie laughed. "Believe me, honey, I'd know that look anywhere. You are already hooked."

Kelly looked at her mom for a moment and then turned her eyes straight ahead. Her mind began to race as she wondered if her mom were right. But how could she be? After all, she didn't even know him yet, and he might not even like her when, and if, they did meet. She smiled as she thought about the possibility of meeting someone new. Her smile quickly faded as she thought, *What if he thinks I'm ugly? Oh, well. I'm not going to worry about it. Jeremy probably won't introduce me to him anyway.*

Kelly's mom pulled up to the front of the school to let her out. "Have a good day, honey. Good luck with the hunk."

Kelly looked at her mom and stuck out her tongue.

"Oh, that's a look I'm sure that the young man would fall in love with."

"Goodbye, Mom!" Kelly stepped out of the car and was greeted by two of her friends.

"Hi, Kelly! Are you still going to the game Friday night? We're playing Westland. They're supposed to be the best team in the league."

"Hi, Sarah! Hi, Traci!"

Traci spoke before Kelly had the chance to answer Sarah's question. "Of course she's going. After all, Michael's playing."

Kelly was sorry that she had shared her thoughts with

her friends. What if nothing worked out? She would be totally embarrassed. "Yes, I'm going but not because of Michael. I just want to support our school."

Sarah laughed. "Your sudden loyalty is real heartwarming, Kelly."

Kelly looked at the two girls. "You know the old saying, 'Be true to your school.'"

The girls looked at each other and then burst into laughter. They were still laughing when they entered the school. The girls were just coming around the corner of the main hallway when Michael flew around the corner and ran into Kelly. The books in her bag tore through the already split seam of her bag and plummeted to the floor. Kelly was too stunned to say anything. Sarah and Traci were smiling and looking first at Kelly and then at Michael.

Michael just looked at Kelly. He had wanted to meet her, but this was not what he'd had in mind. "I'm really sorry. I'm running late. I should have watched where I was going." He bent down and began to pick up her books. Sarah and Traci were hitting each other and rolling their eyes at Kelly. Sarah nodded for Kelly to say something to him, but she was too stunned to think of anything to say. Michael handed Kelly's book bag back to her. He too was at a loss for words. He just looked at her and smiled. "I really am sorry."

As Michael walked away, three young girls were busy giggling. Michael looked back over his shoulder at Kelly.

"Oh my gosh, Kelly! He looked back over his shoulder at you. I think he likes you."

"Sarah, how can you say that? He didn't even say anything to me."

Traci agreed. "When a guy looks over his shoulder at you, he definitely is interested."

"You two have been watching too much TV." The girls watched Michael until he was out of sight. The bell rang, and the girls panicked and began racing for their classroom. Kelly was trying to hold her book bag together; Sarah and Traci were laughing and talking about the first meeting of Michael and Kelly.

▬ ▬ ▬ ▬ ▬ ▬ ▬ ▬

Michael walked in the door to his house just as the phone was ringing. He placed his books on the table and answered the phone. "Hello!"

"Hi, honey. It's me."

"Hi, Mom. I thought you were coming home early today?"

"I was, but we had some paperwork to finish before we could leave, so I'll be a little later than I had planned. That's why I'm calling. I need you to go to the market and pick up something for our dinner."

"Pizza!"

"I swear, Michael, I think you would eat pizza seven days a week if I let you."

Michael smiled. "Probably."

"Just get us a couple of TV dinners. You know what I like. I guess if you really do want pizza, it's alright. I just hope that someday we can live a normal life, with lots of real dinners."

Michael knew that his mom didn't like working late, and he was sorry that she had to do it. His dad's death had really been hard on her. "Mom, it's okay! I would help if you would let me get a job."

"No way, Michael! Your dad and I never wanted you to have to work while you were in high school, and nothing has changed."

"But, Mom!"

"No buts, Michael. We're going to make it, and we are going to do it without you working."

"Just trying to do my part, Mom."

"You just keep doing good in school, Michael. That's enough of a reward for me. I've got to get off of the phone. There's some money in the jar on the shelf above the stove."

"I'll be here when you get home."

"Good! I'll see you later, Michael. I love you."

"I love you too, Mom. Bye!" Michael hung up the phone and went to the stove. As he took the jar off the shelf and took out some money, he noticed that there was very little money left. He shook his head. "Why won't you let me help, Mom?" He put the jar back on the shelf and walked out the door.

Michael never did like going to the store for his mom. It wasn't that he didn't want to do something for her, but he just thought that going to the store was a woman's job. He walked into Clawson's Market and asked someone where the frozen food section was. He headed to the rear of the store, wanting to finish before he ran into anyone from school. He walked around the corner of the aisle and collided with someone. "Excuse me, I—" Kelly! He had just run into Kelly for the second time that day.

Kelly was as startled as Michael was. She just stood there wishing she knew what to say. Michael broke the awkward silence. "I don't believe this. I've run into you twice in one day."

Kelly managed a nervous smile. "That's alright. I don't mind. I mean, you didn't hurt me or anything."

Michael nervously stuck out his hand. "I'm Michael Fredricks."

Kelly shook his hand. "I'm Kelly Carlisle. I've seen you play football." Kelly knew as soon as she had said it that the comment sounded dumb. She was just so nervous she didn't know what to say.

"I've seen you around, too. I hear that you're friends with Jeremy Wethers?"

"Yes, he's in my youth group at church."

Michael had never felt so awkward talking to a girl before. He felt drawn to her but just didn't know what to say. After a very strained silence he said, "Well, I'd better be going. I guess I'll see you again."

"I hope so." Kelly couldn't believe what she had just said. *Nothing like being forward,* she thought. Michael smiled and for the first time noticed her uniform. "Do you work here?"

Kelly smiled. "Yes, I run one of the registers."

Michael grinned. "I guess I'll see you sooner than I

thought then. I've got to pick up something for my mom. She's working late, and I'm just trying to help her out."

Michael couldn't believe that he was trying to make an excuse for being in the store. He just didn't want to give Kelly the wrong impression.

"I think it's sweet that you would do that for your mom. A lot of guys would think it wasn't the macho thing to do. I think it's great that you're not hung up on that."

For the first time Michael was glad that he had to come to the grocery store. Maybe this wasn't so bad after all. Funny how remarks from the right person could change your entire outlook. "I guess I'll see you up front then."

Kelly's heart was racing. Her palms were sweating, and her throat was dry; but she managed to smile and nod her head.

Michael watched Kelly as she walked away until he ran into a stack of cans, almost knocking over the entire display. He laughed, shook his head, and went on to finish his task.

■ ■ ■ ■ ■ ■ ■

Michael had come through Kelly's line and left. Her mind was still racing with things she wished she had said. For some reason, her day had suddenly become much brighter.

Kelly didn't notice her mom standing in her line. "Excuse me, dear."

"Mom! I didn't see you standing there."

Her mom smiled. "That was very obvious. Where in the world was your mind?"

Kelly's smile broadened as she said excitedly, "Mom, he was here!"

"Who was here?"

Kelly couldn't contain her excitement. "Michael! The boy I told you about. The football player!"

Kelly's mom smiled as she remembered their conversation on the way to school. "That football player?"

"Mom, he is so cute! I think he likes me too. He didn't say so, but I can tell. Do you think that's just wishful thinking?"

Connie's heart went out to her daughter as she remembered the first time she had met Kelly's dad. "Not at all, honey, not at all."

Kelly finished ringing up her mom's groceries and told her that she would be home at 9:30. Connie walked toward the door where she paused. Looking back at her daughter she issued a silent prayer, "Please, God, watch over my little girl." She took one last look at Kelly and walked out of the store, leaving behind an excited girl about to embark on a new journey.

CHAPTER 5

"Michael—Michael!"

"I'm sorry, Mom—I was just thinking about my first day at Riverton. It seems like a million years ago."

"You seemed to be lost in another world."

"I guess maybe I was, Mom. A world I wish I could be in today. I sure never thought that I would end up in a wheelchair less than a year later."

"I wish I could take it all away, Michael, but you and I both know that I can't."

Michael watched as his mom moved quickly to the window. He knew she was crying but didn't want him to know. She was trying hard to be strong, but first losing her husband, and now this—it was just too much for her.

Michael tried to assure her, "It's going to be okay, Mom."

Mary knew that things were never going to be right for them again, but she knew his comment was his way of trying to be strong for her. "I don't know who is the biggest liar, you or me."

"What do you mean?"

"We both know that our lives have been changed

forever. Barring some unseen miracle, you'll never be normal again."

"Don't say that, Mom!" Michael's anger took her by surprise. This was the first time he had expressed that emotion, at least in front of her. Michael's voice began to break, and tears began to fill his eyes. "Don't you ever say that again. I'm not giving up. Not now, not tomorrow, never. Don't you ever give up, either. I need your help. I'm down, but I'm not out."

"I'm sorry, honey. I'm just so angry and confused. I don't really know who to be angry with. Should I be angry with God? Your father? I don't know. I just wanted for us to have a fresh start."

"What good is it going to do to be angry with anyone? I just know that if there's any way at all that I can walk again, I'm going to find it. This could have happened anywhere, Mom."

"But it didn't! It happened here, and I'm responsible for bringing you here." Mary caught herself and realized that she was doing more harm than good. She walked to the bed and sat down in the chair beside Michael. She looked around the room as if seeing it for the first time. "Not much of a room, is it?"

Michael was glad for the change of conversation. "No, I guess it's not. I guess when you're stuck in here, you just don't feel good enough to think about it."

"I know what you need! You need that picture of the football player in your room. What's his name? Dick Butkiss?"

"Butkus mom. Dick Butkus, not Butkiss."

"Oh, thank God. I never did like that name. I couldn't figure out why someone would have a name like that."

Michael looked at his mom and started to laugh. Soon she too was caught up in the laughter. They both laughed so hard they cried. "You know, Mom, this really isn't all that funny."

"I know. So why are we laughing so hard?"

"I think we're both too tired to think straight."

Just then a nurse entered the room. "Is everything alright in here?"

"Not really. Get this crazy woman out of here!"

"Everything is fine. My son is just losing his mind, that's all."

"I heard the noise and didn't know if someone was laughing or crying."

Mary said, "At this point, who knows. They say there's a fine line between a genius and an idiot. Maybe that goes for laughing and crying, too."

The nurse smiled, shook her head, and left the room.

"It sure feels good to laugh again, Michael."

"I know. I need you, Mom. I need you to push me. To keep telling me that I can do it—even when it doesn't seem like I can."

"I'll try, honey. I won't make any promises, or say that I won't get discouraged, but I'll try to give you all the help I possibly can. Okay?"

"That's all I ask. I just can't give up. I won't."

"Is this a private party, or can anyone join?"

Michael and his mom looked up. It was Mindy Thomas, the physical therapist assigned to Michael.

"Sure. Come on in!"

"How are you feeling, Michael?"

"Physically or mentally?"

"Both! You can't get any better if you don't have the right attitude."

Michael's mom said, "He'll be fine. He's a very strong young man."

"That's good, because I'm going to work him very hard. No slackers. Okay?" She moved toward Michael's bed. "I've got to make some adjustments to your bed."

Michael and his mom watched as Miss Thomas moved about the bed with precision. She adjusted all of the pulleys and cables that were attached to Michael's body. "Any discomfort?"

"No. It's fine."

"Just let me know if there is, and I'll make some more adjustments. We don't want our star patient to be uncomfortable."

"I'll bet you say that to all of your patients."

Miss Thomas smiled. "Only the special ones, Michael. Only the special ones. Try to get some rest. You're going to need it."

With that Miss Thomas left the room.

"I like her a lot Michael."

"Me, too! If anyone can help me, maybe she can."

"Well, Michael, I do declare. Are you attracted to that young lady?"

Michael looked and saw the sly grin on his mom's face. "Right, Mom. She's probably your age. I don't want an antique."

"You rat! Don't forget, I can take advantage of you right now."

"Not for long, Mom. Not for long."

"I hate to go, honey, but I've got a ton of things to do. I'll be back later tonight." As his mom gathered up her things, Michael reached out and took hold of her arm. "What is it, honey?"

"I love you, Mom."

With a tear in her eye she bent down and kissed him. "I love you too, Michael. With all my heart."

Michael watched as she left. He knew that she blamed herself, but that made him all the more determined to walk again. Michael closed his eyes and was soon in a deep sleep.

"Good evening, young man."

Michael opened his eyes and saw a woman who reminded him very much of his grandmother. He had not seen his grandma for a long time and just now realized how much he missed her.

"I've brought your dinner for you. I hope you're hungry."

"Not really. I haven't done anything to give me an appetite."

"Oh, I know, honey, but you've got to keep up your strength."

"That sounds like something my grandmother would say."

"She sounds like a wise lady to me, honey."
Michael smiled as he thought about his grandmother.

"Yes, ma'am. She is a very wise lady."

"You have a pleasant evening."

"Yes ma'am! You too."

Michael could still hear her cart as she walked into the hall. "I will, dear. God's love shines down on me every day."

Michael turned his eyes toward the window in his room. He noticed the evening rush-hour traffic was moving very slowly. In the distance he could see a passenger jet climbing into the evening sky. *How I wish I could be on that plane,* he thought. *I don't know where I would go, but I wish I were anywhere but here.*

"Hi, Michael!"

Michael knew the voice before he saw her face. It was Kelly. He looked at her and smiled, "Hi, Kelly."

"May I come in?"

"What do you think?"

"I brought you something." She handed him a magazine. "It's this month's issue of Pro Football. At least that's what I think they call it. Jeremy said that you'd like it."

"Thanks. Where is Jeremy anyway? He hasn't been up to see me."

"He's having a hard time dealing with all this."

"Not him, too. It's not his fault. It just happened."

"But it's not fair, Michael. Everyone feels bad about it."

"I don't want people to feel sorry for me, Kelly. Everyone is treating me like I'm never going to be normal again. I'm not going to give up, so don't feel sorry for me."

"I'm sorry, Michael."

"I am too, Kelly. It's just too hard to do this alone. I need all of my friends."

"We'll be there. I promise you we will."

"Okay. Now, why don't you sit down and tell me all about the things going on at school?"

Kelly pulled a package of envelopes from her purse and began to share the cards and letters from all of the kids at school. The time passed quickly, and it was soon time for Kelly to go. She left just as they were announcing the close of visiting hours. Michael could see her car from his window and watched her as she walked to the car. Just before she got in she looked up toward Michael's room and waved. Michael felt tears begin to fill his eyes. They had just begun to develop a good relationship, now he wasn't sure what would happen. What if he couldn't walk again? What if he had to spend the rest of his life in a wheelchair? He couldn't expect Kelly to want to be around a cripple.

Michael turned his face away from the window and fought back the tears. *What if everyone's right?* he thought. *What if I never can walk again?*

Michael lay there listening to the sounds of people moaning, carts squeaking; the sounds of phones ringing, voices in the hall. Suddenly he realized that life went on.

Most people were not aware of Michael Fredricks, let alone the fact that anything had happened to him. He began to feel very much alone. The fact that most of his friends had not come to see him didn't help. He looked out the window into the darkness. He saw the lights of cars moving down the highway, lights in distant homes. Michael turned his eyes back into his room. He stared at the ceiling. Soon his eyes filled with tears. A very frightened young man, with a very uncertain future, cried himself to sleep.

■ ■ ■ ■ ■ ■ ■ ■

The next few weeks were very hard for Michael. The hours of physical therapy took their toll. He thought about how good Mindy would be as a football coach. She worked him harder than any coach he had ever played for. He knew that if he was going to walk again he had to be pushed. Still, sometimes he felt she was too strict.

Kelly's daily visits helped the time pass quickly for him, and soon it was time to go home. Kelly, after her usual visit, had left for the night, and Michael lay looking out the window. He thought about how much he wanted to walk out of the hospital on his own. He knew that was impossible. Still, it would have been great. He thought about his mom and all of the added burden she was facing taking care of him. That was the last thing he had ever wanted. She never complained, but he still felt guilty. He wished there was something he could do to change the situation. He made a silent vow to his mom to once again be able to take care of her.

Michael looked at the clock in his room and realized that in less than twenty-four hours he would be home. He faced that thought with excitement and fear. He spent the rest of the night trying to get the sleep that he knew would never come.

CHAPTER 6

The rain had been falling all night, but the clouds were beginning to break up, and the sun was shining through the clouds. *What a beautiful sunrise,* Michael thought.

He was busy taking in the scene when he looked up and saw Miss Thomas, the physical therapist, standing at the door. "Nice morning to get out of this place, isn't it?"

"I can't wait."

"Michael, I know that you expected to make more progress than you have made, but trust me, it's only been a little over four weeks since your accident. You have made excellent progress. I don't want to discourage you, but I've got to be honest. You may never be completely whole. You broke your back in a very bad place. Not that there are any good places, but it's going to take time, and a miracle wouldn't hurt either.

"My mom said the same thing."

"Miracles do happen, Michael. But God is the one who makes that decision."

"I don't even know that I believe in God. Besides, if He does exist, He might not even know who I am."

"Believe me, He knows who you are."

"Good morning!"

Michael's mom walked into the room. "You two look like you're having a real serious discussion. There's nothing wrong, is there?"

"No, not at all. I was just telling Michael not to get discouraged. He still has a lot of physical therapy to go through. He can't give up yet."

"I'm not about to give up," Michael said confidently.

"Good! I've brought you a list of do's and don'ts, Mrs. Fredricks. There are some exercises that you can help him do. They're pretty simple, but also very important."

"I can't thank you enough for all of things you have done for my son. You've been a tremendous help."

"It's my job, and my pleasure, Mrs. Fredricks."

"Please, call me 'Mary.'"

Miss Thomas smiled. "Thank you, Mary. I'll do that. Well, I'd best be on my way. I've got some other patients to see. I'll see you in three days when you come in for your first of many visits."

"Not too many, I hope." Michael smiled. "Nothing personal."

"Goodbye, Miss Thomas."

"Goodbye Mrs. Fredricks. I mean, Mary. See you, Michael."

"Okay, Mindy."

"Mindy? On a first-name basis, are we? I knew there was something to worry about."

"Right, Mom. Let's get out of here. I want to see my room again."

"I'll go get the nurse, and she can help us get you into the car. I'm afraid I've got a lot to learn, too."

"Yeah! It's a scary thought knowing that you're going to have to depend on your mom to help you go to the bathroom."

"It's nothing I haven't done before. I'll go get the nurse, unless, of course, you want Mindy to help instead."

"Wipe that silly grin off your face and get the nurse. You're wasting time."

The ride home was pleasant for Michael. He felt as if he had been let out of jail. He opened the window and tried to absorb as much of the fresh air as he could. "Man, it feels great to be out of there."

"I'll bet it does, honey. Kelly's dad is coming over to meet us. Just in case we need help getting you into the house."

"Mom, I'm not going to bother a lot of people. I've still got my upper body strength. Besides, that's one of the things Mindy taught me. How to get in and out of the car."

They pulled into the drive, and Mr. Carlisle was waiting for them. Mary pulled the car to a stop in the driveway, and Mr. Carlisle came around to Michael's side of the car. He opened the door and greeted him. "How are you doing, Michael?"

"Fine, Mr. Carlisle."

"How can I help?"

"If you get the wheelchair out of the trunk, I can get out myself."

"Are you sure?"

"Sure. I've practiced it a hundred times."

"Okay!" Mr. Carlisle took the keys from Michael's mom, opened the trunk, and took out the wheelchair. He rolled it up to Michael's door and positioned it for him. Michael tried to remember everything Mindy had taught him. He grabbed the frame of the door and the wheelchair and swung himself into the seat. Michael grinned broadly as he enjoyed the victory of overcoming one small hurdle.

"You made that look easy, Michael."

"Thank you, Mr. Carlisle." It was at that point that Michael noticed the ramp that had been built on the front of the house. "Where did that come from?"

"Mr. Carlisle built it for us."

"Jeremy Wethers helped me."

"Great! Jeremy doesn't come to see me in the hospital, but he helps build a ramp that I'm not going to need for long."

Mr. Carlisle could sense Michael's anger and tried to reassure him. "It's just temporary, Michael. We built it so that we could take it apart easily."

Michael saw the ramp as one more sign that no one believed he was going to get better. He determined in his heart to help them tear down that ramp.

Inside, Michael looked around the house as if seeing it for the first time.

"Do you need me for anything else, Mary?"

"No! Thank you very much for all of your help. Do I owe you anything?"

"No! Not at all. It's been my pleasure."

"But I haven't even paid you for the wood to build the ramp."

"Jeremy and I took care of it. You don't owe me a thing."

"Thank you very much. Please tell Kelly to come by any time."

"Thanks. I'm sure she'll spend a lot of time here. You take care of yourself, Michael. If you folks need anything at all just give me a call. Anytime, night or day."

Mary walked him to the door and thanked him again for his help. She closed the door and turned to speak to Michael, but he was gone. She walked back to his room and found him sitting there, just soaking it all in.

"I sure missed this room, Mom."

"I certainly missed having you in this room. I'll fix us some lunch. Are you very hungry?"

"Yeah, I am! Thanks."

Michael looked at his room. There was something wrong. Then he realized what it was: it was too clean. He was used to having what he called the lived-in look. As he looked around, he saw his baseball bat and shoes standing in the corner. His trophies were neatly lined up on the dresser. His football jersey from his old school was hanging on the mirror of his dresser. Then his eyes caught sight of the picture of Dick Butkus. He began to smile when he thought of his mom's comment about Dick Butkiss.

"Michael, there's someone here to see you."

Michael turned around to see Mr. Bryant, his football coach. Michael was glad to see him. "Hi, Coach!"

"How are you doing, son?"

"I'm doing better, sir, now that I'm home. Come on in and sit down, Coach."

Coach Bryant moved to the bed and sat down. He looked around the room and smiled. "Looks like I thought it might, except for one thing."

"I know." Then they both said, "It's too clean."

Michael laughed. "My mom took advantage of my being gone. It shouldn't take me too long to whip it back in shape."

"Good choice of words, Michael."

"How are you doing, Coach? You starting to get ready for next year yet?"

"You bet! One season ends, but then you have to begin to get ready for the next one. If I didn't love it so much, I'd give it up. It's just too much work sometimes. Enough about me. I want to know how you're holding up."

"I'm starting to get some strength back."

"Will you—"

Michael knew by the long pause that Coach Bryant was having difficulty dealing with his injury, just like everyone else.

"Walk again? I believe I will. Maybe no one else does, but I definitely do."

"I'm glad you have that attitude. If anything can get you through, a strong determination will. By the way, I was wondering if you would be interested in helping me coach next year?"

"I don't know if I'll be able to walk that soon, Coach."

"I know, but you've got a great head for football, and it's something you could even do from your wheelchair, or on crutches."

Michael paused and then looked at Coach Bryant. "Let me think about it, Coach. I mean, I'd love to do it, but I just don't know if I can. Do you know what I mean?"

"More than you may know. I know that you have noticed my limp. I don't tell this story to many people, but I think it may be appropriate here."

Coach Bryant took a deep breath and looked deep into Michael's eyes. Michael felt a closeness to Coach Bryant that he never shared with very many people.

"I was sixteen, and in the best shape of my life. I was the starting center for my high-school football team. I had a lot of college scouts watching me already, just like you. My best friend and I were cruising, looking for girls. We had left town and were going out to the old creek we used to swim in. My friend loved his car and loved to go fast. We came to a sharp curve in the road, but Jerry was going too fast to make it. He lost control, and we left the road. Jerry was thrown out of the car and into a tree. I was pinned in the wreckage.

"I didn't know until much later that Jerry hadn't made it. He was killed instantly. I broke my leg in three places. They had to put pins in it, and I went through a lot of therapy, but it never healed completely. Needless to say my career in football came to an abrupt end. I finished college and landed my first job as a coach. I loved the game and felt that it was the only way I could still be involved. I've never regretted the decision. I've been able to help some fine young men find their way into college football. I guess I'm telling you this story because I want you to know that there is still hope, even if you're not made whole."

"Thanks, Coach. It does help, but I am going to get better."

"I hope so, son. The offer still stands to help me coach. You could really help my defense."

"I may take you up on that."

"I hope so, Michael." Coach Bryant stood up to leave. "It was good to see you. You take good care of yourself. Try to get this room back in shape, will you?"

"You bet, Coach. Thanks for coming by." Michael watched as Coach Bryant walked out. He was glad he had told him about his injury. Still, he couldn't help feeling a little sorry for him. Who knows how great a player he could have been.

Michael was looking at the magazine Kelly had given him. He hadn't felt much like looking at it until now.

"Hey, Michael!"

Michael looked up to see Jeremy Wethers. "Hey, Jeremy. What's up?"

"Look, I'm sorry I haven't been around till now. I just couldn't deal with seeing you like this. It was me who was driving the boat."

"I'm doing fine, thanks. How are you?"

"What?"

"Look, Jeremy. What I don't need is one more person feeling like it was their fault that I got hurt. I was the one who wanted to go skiing. I was the one who tried to show off for Kelly. I never said that before, but I did want to show Brad that I could ski as good as he could. I didn't want to look bad in front of Kelly. So lay off the pity party. Okay?"

Jeremy stood there looking at Michael. Then he dropped his head, was quiet for a moment, and turned and walked away. Michael stared at the empty doorway. Maybe he had been too hard on him. He wished he had kept his mouth shut. It really was good to see him. Jeremy reappeared at the door. He smiled, "Hey! How are you feeling?"

Michael smiled, "Get in here, you clown."

"I love you, too."

"Look, I'm sorry. I just don't want anyone to feel bad for me. I worry enough for all of us."

"No problem. I'm sorry I didn't come sooner. It wasn't like I wasn't thinking about you."

"That's cool. I probably wasn't much company to anyone anyway. So it's probably for the best. Anyhow the important thing is you're here now. By the way, thanks for the ramp. I hate to make you go through all that work for nothing. I won't be needing it for long."

"Man, that's great! Then you're going to walk again?"

"I sure don't intend to stay in this wheelchair all my life. One day soon I'll take you on in a game of football."

Jeremy looked at him, "How are you going to do that?"

"Computer football, dummy. The other will come later. I'll whip your butt either way."

"Fat chance, linebacker. They don't even teach you guys how to think, do they? I heard they just feed you raw meat."

"At least we don't spend all our time in front of the mirror. That's all you pretty-boy quarterbacks do, isn't it?"

"Come on, boy. Put your money where your mouth is."

Michael and Jeremy moved to the computer in his room, and were soon doing what they did best. Trash talking each other.

CHAPTER 7

Sitting at her desk, supposedly working, but with her mind a million miles away, Mary Fredricks sat staring out the window, thinking of the events of the past few weeks. She couldn't believe all that had taken place. She could see Michael making very little progress. His upper body was getting stronger, but his legs were still not working.

She wondered if there was anything else she could do.

"Penny for your thoughts."

Mary looked up. It was Judy Phillips.

"Hi! I was just thinking about everything that's happened to me in the last two years."

"It hasn't been easy for you; that's for sure."

"It hasn't been easy for Michael either. He had so many plans for the future. He was just starting to date a lovely girl. Now this happened. I just don't understand life sometimes, Judy."

"Welcome to the club. Just when you think things are going good for you, something happens."

I've been thinking. Maybe I need to move. You know, take Michael someplace where they have better facilities. A place where he can get the help he needs to get better."

"You said yourself that he may never walk again. Besides, that takes a lot of money."

"Michael's father left us some insurance money. Maybe I should spend that. I know it wouldn't be enough, but I've got to do something."

"Maybe it's too soon to do something like that. Are you certain Michael would want to move again? You said yourself that he was just starting to date a girl. He has made some new friends. Maybe this isn't the right time to try to disrupt his world again."

"I suppose you're right. I just feel so helpless. Maybe I should talk to him about it."

"You know him much better than I do. Still, you may want to think about it some more."

"I guess we'd better get back to work. I sure can' t afford to lose my job right now. Thanks for letting me bare my soul."

"You're welcome. See you at lunch time."

The drive home that evening seemed unusually long to Mary. She had to stop at the grocery to pick up some things she needed, but the traffic didn't seem to want to cooperate. She pulled into the parking lot, and found a spot close to the door. *Finally!* she thought. *Something went right today.*

She walked into the store, found a cart, and began the arduous task of buying groceries. She was trying extra hard to buy things that Michael enjoyed.

"Hi, Mrs. Fredricks!"

Mary looked around and saw Kelly. "Hi, Kelly! How are you doing?"

"I'm fine. How's Michael?"

"I think he's doing okay, dear. He doesn't complain much. He really never has. I'm very lucky that he has that sort of disposition."

"I'll be over later, if that's okay."

"Of course it is, Kelly. You're welcome anytime."

Kelly paused for a moment as if searching for the right words. "May I ask you something?"

"Of course. What is it?"

"Does Michael not want me to come around anymore?"

"What in the world would make you ask that?"

"Sometimes he just doesn't seem glad to see me, that's all. I mean, he treats me alright, but I don't know how to describe it."

"I know that he likes you very much. I think that he just doesn't want you to waste your time hanging around him."

"Why in the world would he feel like that?"

"Kelly, Michael had a lot of plans for his future. Now he may be forced to change those plans completely. I think he is afraid, at least deep down, that he will never walk again. He knows that you're still healthy and strong, and he wants you to be able to do all the things he may not be able to do."

"I like Michael, Mrs. Fredricks. Not for what he can do for me, but just because I do. I still like him as much as I ever did, maybe more. He seems so strong. I know that it may all be going slow, but at least he's trying to beat this thing. A lot of guys I know wouldn't try that hard. That's something that I admire about him."

"Why don't you tell him what you've told me? Maybe he'll understand just how special you really are."

"Thank you, Mrs. Fredricks. I guess I'd better get out of here. Mom sent me to the store to get some things for dinner tonight. If I don't get back, I may not get to eat."

"Be careful, Kelly. I'll see you later."

As Kelly walked away she looked back over her shoulder. "Tell Michael I'll be over later."

"I'll tell him."

"Oh! Tell him that I'm praying for him, too."

"Just keep on praying, dear. We need all the help we can get."

"Bye!"

"Goodbye."

Mary watched Kelly for a moment, thinking about how lucky Michael was to have found a girl like her. *If only this hadn't happened,* she thought. *If only.* She turned and walked to the checkout. The pain in her heart brought a tear to her eye, as she thought about the young man that she loved so much. For the first time she realized how much Michael reminded her of her husband. They both shared that same inner strength. A strength that she wished she possessed at this time.

— — — — — — —

Michael saw his mom pull into the driveway. He shut off the television. Wasn't much on anyway. He watched as his mom took the groceries out of the car. He wished so much that he could go out there to help her. *She looks tired,* he thought. *This whole ordeal has been just as hard on her as on me. She has to do all the things that I used to do for her.*

"Not for long," he whispered. "Not for long, Mom."

Mary walked through the door with her arms loaded with bags. "Hi, honey! Did you have a good day?"

"Same old stuff, Mom."

Mary took the groceries into the kitchen. "I ran into Kelly today."

"Did you hurt her?"

Mary came back into the room with a strange look on her face. "Did I what?"

"You said you ran in to her, right?"

"Yes."

"Did you hurt her? Duh! Think about it, Mom. Ran into her!"

Mary thought for a moment. "You're terrible, Michael."

"And you're getting old. You don't even understand a good joke when you hear one."

"Maybe I just didn't hear a good one, Mr. Smarty Britches."

"Smarty Britches? Man, you are getting old."

"Cute, Michael, real cute. Why don't you come into

the kitchen for a moment? I've got something I want to talk to you about."

Michael wheeled himself into the kitchen. "What is it?"

Mary paused from unpacking the groceries, moved to the table, pulled out a chair, and sat down. "I've been reading about a hospital in Boston. They have a real good physical therapy unit there. They're also experimenting with some new surgery techniques."

"So you want me to go there. Right?"

"I want us to go there."

"What about your job?"

"I'll get one there."

"Wait a minute!" Michael began to become very angry. "You can't be serious. You just moved us here a year ago. I didn't want to move then, and I sure don't want to move now. Moving won't change a thing, Mom. I've got friends here now, and I like it here."

"It wouldn't have to be permanent. We could come back when you get better."

"No!"

"Please, Michael, don't be angry. I just want what's best for you."

"If you do, then don't move me again. I'll do just fine here. I'll talk to Mindy, and if she says she thinks it might help to go there for visit, I'll go. But I will not move! Not again. Please."

"Michael, I want you to have a normal life again. I want you to have a wife and children. I want to be a grandmother."

"Don't you think I want those things too? But I just don't need any more to deal with. I'm trying to keep a good attitude. Just let me deal with things one day at a time."

Mary reached out and took Michael's hand. "Please don't be angry with me."

"I'm not. I'm as scared as you are. We have to get through this, and we will."

"That seems like something I should be saying to you."

Michael smiled. "You told me when Dad died that I had to be the man of the house. I'm still trying to do that. I want you to be happy too. Sometimes I get real angry because your life is just as screwed up as mine. I have to depend on you for things I don't like to depend on you for."

"I don't mind."

"I know that, but I do. I want us both to have a real life."

"I love you, Michael."

"I love you too, Mom. Now fix me something to eat. I'm starved."

Mary smiled. "I guess some things never change do they?"

"Not where food's concerned," Michael joked.

"Get out of my way then. I've got work to do." She watched as Michael wheeled himself out of the kitchen. She had been so busy with her life that she didn't notice that her little boy had grown up.

CHAPTER 8

Michael was sitting in the living room watching TV. Actually, the television might have been on, but his mind was somewhere else. He was thinking about the proposal his mom had made the day before. He knew she meant well, but the last thing he needed right now was more change. The pain of losing his mobility was enough to deal with. *I hope I didn't hurt her feelings,* he thought. *But I've got to be able to win this battle right here, in my new hometown.*

Michael was surprised to hear himself call Riverton his new hometown. But, in spite of everything that had happened, he really did like the town and its people. All of his teachers had volunteered to send his work home with friends. Some of them had even agreed to tutor him if he needed it. This was one time that he was glad that his school work came easy for him.

Scanning the channels, he happened upon a baseball game. He watched as the players moved about the field, wishing he could still be playing. It was times like these that he felt the full weight of what had happened to him. The frustration, the helplessness, seemed to overwhelm him. He felt himself begin to cry but fought back the tears. He had made himself a promise not to cry anymore. He felt that it was a sign of weakness, a sign that he was giving up and accepting his fate.

He changed the channel, hoping to find something that he could watch. The days of sitting in front of the television were beginning to take their toll on him. Even before he was injured, he had never really liked watching too much TV. Most of the programs, except for sports, seemed kind of boring. He enjoyed being active and running with his friends too much to spend time in front of the television.

Michael was still trying to find something to watch when he heard a car enter his driveway. He knew that it was too early for his mom to be coming home. He heard doors opening and closing, and the sound of voices. Turning off the TV, he rolled over to the living room window and opened the drapes. Looking out of the window, he saw Coach Bryant, Coach Fuller, and half of the football team walking toward the house. Curious, he rolled to the door and opened it.

Coach Bryant was the first to speak. "How are you doing, Michael?"

Michael, still curious as to the purpose of their visit, said hesitantly, "I'm doing okay, Coach. I guess I'm just a little surprised to see so many of you here at once."

Coach Fuller smiled. "We have a little surprise for you."

"A surprise?" Michael's mind was racing, trying to figure out what sort of surprise they could have for him.

Coach Bryant, looking at Michael, began to speak. As he did, Michael noticed tears beginning to fill the big man's eyes. "Michael, we as a team wanted to show you how much you have meant to us and to our school's football program this year. We all believe that you have the strength and determination you're going to need to beat this problem you're facing. To that end, we wanted to do something to help you achieve your goal. So we held a team meeting and decided that there was one thing you didn't have that you might need."

Coach Bryant looked toward the pickup parked at the end of the line of cars in the driveway. He motioned to the boys standing behind it. He saw Jeremy and the others begin to carry boxes to the front porch. He was even more confused than he was before. What in the world could be in those boxes that could help him? One by one, the boys piled their boxes on the porch in front of Michael. Jeremy was grinning from ear to ear.

"What is this?" Michael asked.

Coach Fuller smiled. "Why don't we let Jeremy tell you?"

Michael looked at Jeremy, who was dying to do just that. "It's a multi-station exercise gym. You can do all kinds of exercises with it."

Michael couldn't believe his eyes. "I can't believe you guys did this. I don't know what to say."

Coach Bryant smiled. "Just use it to get better. That's all the thanks we need."

Michael felt tears begin to fill his own eyes. *So much for promising myself not to cry,* he thought.

Coach Bryant asked if it was alright for them to take the equipment in and set it up for him. Michael, a little overwhelmed, said, "Sure, Coach. We've got a spare bedroom. We can set it up in there."

Michael watched as, one by one, the pieces were carried inside. He was too busy checking out the boys' cargo to notice that his mom had pulled up in front of the house. She got out of the car and made her way to the front porch, anxious to find out what all of the cars were doing in her driveway. "Michael! What in the world is going on here?"

"You won't believe it, Mom! The guys on the football team went together to buy me a new exercise machine. It's unbelievable!"

Mary walked onto the porch and greeted Coach Bryant. She saw a look in her son's eyes that made her feel very guilty for even suggesting that they move. She knew without a doubt that they were in the best place for him. She looked at Coach Bryant. "I guess I don't know what to say, except thank you very much."

Coach Bryant smiled warmly. "Michael's reaction was enough thanks for us, Mrs. Fredricks."

Mary smiled. "Please, call me Mary."

Coach Bryant told Michael that he'd better get inside and supervise the set-up. He quickly took his advice and headed for the bedroom. Coach Bryant placed his hand on Mary's shoulder. She turned, trying to hold back the tears.

"You have every right to be very proud of that young

man, Mrs. Fredricks. I mean, Mary. He's won the heart of a lot of people in a very short period of time."

Mary wiped away a tear that she couldn't control. "I am, Coach Bryant. I only wish that his dad were here to see him."

"I hope we didn't do something that we shouldn't have done. I guess we should have asked if it would be alright."

Mary smiled warmly. "No, sir! You did something very right, and I'm grateful to you, and to the rest of the team. He has a look in his eyes right now that I wasn't sure I'd ever see again."

Coach Bryant opened the door and made a grand gesture to Mary. Bowing, he said, "Shall we join the festivities?"

She smiled and curtsied. "Thank you, sir."

The noise and laughter was overwhelming when Mary and Coach Bryant entered the room. The boys had boxes and paper thrown all over the place. Right in the middle of the whole mess sat Michael. Beside him was Coach Fuller looking at a stack of papers in his hand. Coach Bryant looked at him and said, "Let me guess. Those must be the directions for this puzzle."

Coach Fuller glanced up at him and smiled. "You guessed it! Should we do it right and read them? Or should we do the manly thing and throw them aside?"

Coach Bryant looked at the pile of steel lying off to one side. "I think this is one time when we definitely need to read the directions."

Michael watched, laughed, and tried to supervise for

the next couple of hours, as piece by piece the machine began to take shape. When it was finally assembled, they all stood back and admired their accomplishment. Coach Bryant, arms folded, was the first to speak. "Gentlemen! Not a bad job, if I do say so myself."

Michael tried to make his way through the maze of paper and cardboard as he surveyed his new prize possession. "Man! I still can't believe that you guys did this for me. With this thing, I'll be back in shape in no time."

Coach Fuller walked over to Michael and knelt down beside him. He was silent for a moment and then looked at him. "We just wanted you to know that we believe in you. You always gave a hundred and ten percent for the team. We just wanted to return the favor."

Michael looked around the room at the group of young men who, at that moment, meant more to him than he could possibly tell them. He looked at Jeremy, who was beaming with pride. "Thanks, buddy. I owe you one. Thanks to all of you. You'll never know how much this means to me."

Coach Bryant smiled. "Just show everyone how tough you are, Michael. We want to see you back on your feet again."

Michael smiled. "I'll do my best, Coach."

Coach Fuller stood up and made the announcement that no one wanted to hear. "I guess it's time to clean up this mess and get out of here."

Mary quickly interjected. "Don't worry about it. After

everything you've done, the least I can do is clean up the mess."

That remark brought a hearty round of cheers from all of the young men. But Coach Bryant quickly put an end to their joy. "Come on, guys. If we all take a piece, we can clear this up in one trip."

The boys mumbled and complained but knew all too well that they couldn't argue with the coach. Each boy grabbed a piece of trash and filed out of the room, saying goodbye to Michael as they left. Michael watched as one by one they walked out. Mary went with them to show them where they could put the trash. The only ones remaining were the two coaches, Jeremy, and Michael. Coach Fuller was the first to speak. "If you need anything at all, Michael, please don't hesitate to ask."

"Thanks, Coach! I know that you mean it, and I will. Honest."

The two coaches said goodbye to Michael and left.

Jeremy looked at Michael. "Pretty wild! Huh?"

Michael shook his head in agreement. "Yeah, Jeremy, it really is."

Jeremy stuck out his hand and Michael grabbed it. They shook hands and stared at each other for a moment. Then Jeremy said goodbye and left the room.

Michael sat back in his chair and stared at the machine before him. His mind began to race as he considered the possibilities this machine could present. He couldn't wait to tell Kelly and Mindy. He knew that he would have to have Mindy come out and show him how to get on and off of the different positions, but he knew she wouldn't mind. Michael was deep in thought when he heard Kelly's voice.

"Is it all right if I come in?"

Michael turned quickly and smiled at his welcomed guest. "Sure! Come on in." He sat back proudly in his chair and pointed with pride at his newest possession. "Can you believe this?"

Kelly walked around the machine and looked at Michael. "It looks great! But I'm just not sure what it is."

Michael laughed. He had forgotten that Kelly really wasn't into working out. "It's a multi-station exercise machine. I can do all kinds of stuff with this thing. The most important thing is that it's going to help me get out of this wheelchair I'm stuck in."

"Your mom sure was excited when she saw me coming. I didn't really understand what she was trying to tell me, but she said you would explain."

Michael began to tell Kelly everything that had taken place. She agreed that it was unbelievable that his friends would do this. Michael didn't realize that he was rambling, until he saw that faraway look in Kelly's eyes that said she was losing interest. He smiled at her. "I'm sorry. I guess I'm a little too excited. I didn't mean to bore you."

"I'm not bored. I've just got something else on my mind."

Michael's curiosity was stirred, as he wondered what could be so important to her. "What is it? Is something wrong?"

Kelly smiled, sat down on the floor next to Michael, and

stared at the new machine. He could sense her uneasiness but didn't want to make her even more uncomfortable. Finally, she looked at him and tried to find the words she was looking for.

"Have you ever heard of Billy Graham?" Michael smiled and nodded his head. "He's coming to the stadium on the campus of Ohio State University in Columbus next week. I was just wondering if you would ride up there with me. My mom and dad could pick you up."

Michael was ready for anything but this. He sat silently for a moment. He looked at Kelly and could tell by the look in her eyes that this was very important to her. He didn't want to hurt her, but he didn't even like going to church, let alone going to a big stadium full of church people. "I don't know, Kelly. I've never been to anything like that before."

"Neither have I! I just thought it might be fun."

"I'm sorry, Kelly. But I have a hard time associating church with fun."

Kelly could sense his reluctance but didn't want to give up too easily. "He really is interesting, honest. Thursday night is youth night, and he's going to have a special guest there just for us."

"Do I have to say 'yes' right now?"

Kelly smiled. "That would be nice. But, no, I guess not. Just don't say 'no' yet either. Just think about it. Please."

"I will. But I'm not going to promise anything. Okay?"

Kelly smiled, believing in her heart that she knew what his answer would be. "Deal!"

Michael quickly moved to change the subject. "Have you heard from Jeff lately?"

"I got a card from him yesterday. He said he's enjoying his trip, but he's homesick."

"Yeah! I got the same message in a card Monday. You know, it's funny, but he never mentions my accident. Has he said anything to you?"

Kelly could tell that Jeff's lack of curiosity hurt Michael. "No! But I think I understand what he's going through. He's like the rest of us. He just doesn't know what to say. I know that he was as scared as any of us were that day. He called me the day after the accident and told me he hated to leave, but the trip was already planned."

"I guess I just expect too much from people sometimes."

Kelly's heart went out to Michael. "I really do believe that he cares a great deal."

Michael sat back in his chair and stared straight ahead. Kelly watched silently, wishing she could get inside his head and know his thoughts. Finally, Michael looked at her and said, "You know, this really is a great machine."

Kelly smiled, looked at the new equipment, and said, "You're right. It really is."

CHAPTER 9

Michael opened his eyes, and turned his head to look at the clock on his dresser. It was seven o'clock. He laid his head back on his pillow and placed his right arm over his eyes to shield them from the light coming through the open drapes. His thoughts began to drift back to the events of the previous day. The thoughtfulness of his coaches and team- mates. The joy on his mom's face. The look on Kelly's face as she tried to get excited about something she didn't understand. He felt very grateful to have friends like these.

He looked at the picture of Dick Butkus hanging on his wall and smiled. "You'd like this machine, Mr. Butkus. It's a machine for real men."

Michael heard his mom closing her bedroom door and knew that she was getting ready for work. Every time he heard her leave the house on her way to work he felt guilty. He wished he could make her load lighter, but all he had succeeded in doing was creating more of a burden for her. These were the times when he really questioned the existence of a god. If there were, he wondered why anyone would have to suffer pain or death. He was deep in thought when he heard his mom's voice.

"Are you awake, Michael?"

Michael turned and smiled at his mom. She was standing at the door. The morning light from the living room window made her dress glow, silhouetting her body.

"You look like an angel."

Mary walked into the room and sat down on his bed. "Well, as you can clearly see, I am definitely not an angel."

Michael lovingly touched her cheek and smiled. "You are to me."

Mary playfully hit him. "Don't you know it's not nice to make fun of your mother?"

Michael grabbed his arm as if in pain. "Don't you know it's not nice to beat up your kids?"

Mary folded her arms and scowled playfully at Michael. "So, young man, what time did the young lady go home last night?"

Michael came back with his Mr. Innocent look. "I really don't know, Mom. I'm sure it was very early."

Mary unfolded her arms and leaned back on Michael's bed. She looked at him and smiled lovingly. "She is a delightful young lady." Her smile broadened into an all-out grin as she said, "I think that the young woman is quite taken with you."

Michael threatened to shove her out of bed. "I think that you think too much."

"She really does care about you. You can see it in her

face. She just lights up when you're around or when I run into her at the market and she asks about you."

The smile on Michael's face suddenly faded, and he turned his face away. Mary sat up, took his face in her hand and tenderly turned it toward hers. "What is it, Michael? What's wrong?"

The pain on his face placed a heavy burden on Mary's heart. She had seen that look too many times recently. "Why would she want me now, Mom? Until I can get myself together I'll be useless to her. Who knows how long that will take? It could take weeks, months, or even years for me to get better."

Frustrated, Mary struggled for words that could comfort him. She longed to be able to give him something to hold on to, some ray of sunshine, but she too was filled with doubt and uncertainty. "If Kelly is the young lady I think she is, you're not going to be able to get rid of her. I have the feeling that she's determined to see you through this."

"Mom! Can I ask you something?"

"You know the answer to that."

Michael re-positioned himself on the bed and placed his arms behind his head. "Have you ever been to a Billy Graham meeting before?"

Mary shook her head. "No! I never have. I've seen them on TV, but never in person. Why do you ask?"

"Kelly asked me to go to one next week. It's in the OSU Stadium. I don't know what to tell her."

Mary looked at her watch. "I've got to go; I'm going to be late." She stood to her feet and looked at Michael. "I wish I could make that decision for you, but I can't. If you care for someone, sometimes you do things just because they make that person happy. I think it's very important to Kelly to have you there. I guess you have to decide if what she wants is important to you." She reached out and flipped Michael's hair and smiled. "I'm sure that you'll make the right decision. I'll see you later."

Michael watched as his mom left the room. He then lay back and fixed his eyes on a spot on the ceiling. He began to think about what his mom had said. He knew that Kelly was becoming more important to him each day. He just wasn't sure that he should let himself get too close. Things could get very complicated in his life, and he didn't know if he could stand the added strain of trying to build a relationship.

Michael thought about the strain on his mom. The burden of working a full-time job, taking care of all of the chores, and taking care of a handicapped son. Michael hated that word. Handicapped! It filled him with anger and fear. He hated being so much of a burden on his mom! She never got to do anything for herself! He wondered if she ever wanted to go out with the girls at work. She never said anything, but maybe he should suggest it sometime. She might enjoy getting away from everything for a little while. He made up his mind to talk to her about it.

He heard the clock in the living room strike the half hour and remembered that Mindy was coming. His mom had called her about the new machine Michael had been given and asked her if she would come over to check it out. She told her she would come and bring someone with her who could help by installing support bars in various places on the machine.

Michael swung his legs out of bed and maneuvered himself into his wheelchair. He had no sooner made the transition from the bed to the chair when he heard the doorbell ring.

He quickly made his way to the door and greeted his guests. Mindy introduced Michael to John Taylor, an occupational therapist. Michael was always glad to see Mindy. There was just something special about her. He wasn't sure what it was, but he felt very drawn to her. Michael led the way into the spare room where his new equipment was located. He felt a wave of pride embrace him as they entered the room. Mindy smiled. "I'm impressed! This is a very nice piece of equipment."

He watched as Mindy and John surveyed the new machine. John studied the different positions and made notations on a pad he was carrying. He told Mindy that he would get the things he needed from the van and walked out of the room. Mindy looked at Michael.

"How are things going for you?"

"I guess I'm doing okay. I feel kinda helpless."

Mindy had heard that statement a hundred times before, but it had never affected her more than it did now. Michael was too young to have such a devastating injury. He had been a healthy young man with his whole life ahead of him, but now she too was uncertain of the final outcome. She wanted to give him some encouraging words but chose her words carefully. She knew that, as

Michael's therapist, he would cling to almost anything she'd say, good or bad. She sat down beside Michael and looked at the new machine. "This new equipment is definitely a step in the right direction. The more you can exercise the better chance you have for healing. I can only be with you for a small percentage of the time, but you can work on this thing anytime you feel like it. Just one word of caution! Don't try to overdo it. Your body is the best messenger as to what it will take. Learn to listen to it. If you don't feel strong enough, don't push it."

Michael looked at Mindy. He could see confidence in her. The way she carried herself. The way she talked. He was glad she was his therapist. She was easy to talk to. "If I don't know anything else, I know that I'm determined to get my life back. I hate what this has done to me, to my mom. I'll work as hard as I have to."

Mindy could see why Michael had been so successful at sports. He had the kind of determination that it took to be a winner. "Just don't expect too much too soon. That's a dangerous trap to fall into. If you get discouraged too soon, and you will get discouraged, you will more than likely give up. I just don't want you to do that. Okay?"

Michael smiled. "Sure! No problem."

Just then John entered the room with a bag full of tools and parts. He wasted no time getting to his project. He set down his package and began to install the bars Michael could use to move about on his new equipment. Michael and Mindy sat silently and watched as he skillfully completed his task.

John finished tightening the last bolt and stood back.

He surveyed his work like a master craftsman who had just finished one of the greatest works of his life. He looked at Michael. "Never hurts to check everything twice. I don't want to get a phone call to come over here and pull you out of this machine." John's confidence in his own abilities was obvious, and Michael understood why Mindy had chosen him.

Mindy stood up and walked over to the new equipment, and for the next hour, she and John walked Michael through every station, showing him how to get on and off each one. They helped him on and off, again and again, until they were certain that he could do it safely.

John packed up his tools and said goodbye to Michael. He told Mindy he would wait for her in the van. Michael smiled and looked at Mindy. "He seems to know what he's doing."

"He's the best." Mindy picked up her purse and walked over to where Michael was sitting. "How do you feel? You look a little tired."

Michael nodded his head in agreement. "I am tired! I feel like I used to after football practice."

Mindy smiled. "Get used to it! It doesn't get any easier. You up to it?"

"You bet I am!" Michael said confidently.

"Good!" Mindy smiled, said goodbye, and walked out of the room.

Michael listened as Mindy closed the door. He heard the van start and pull out of the driveway. He looked at the bars John had installed. He moved around the machine and studied every inch of it. He took hold of one of the bars. "You and I are going to spend a lot of time together. I'm going to work the chrome right off you."

"Well, folks, he's finally flipped out. He's now talking to a machine."

Startled, Michael turned and saw Jeremy standing in the doorway with an ornery grin on his face. "Jeremy! You scared me to death! I didn't hear you come in."

Jeremy walked in and sat down on one of the benches on the new equipment. He looked at Michael and smiled. "You always talk to yourself?"

"It's better conversation than anything I get from you." Michael loved it when Jeremy came around. He knew he could count on him to liven things up. "I've never known a quarterback who was all that smart."

"You're lucky that I'm a nice guy, or I'd come over there and kick your butt."

Michael laughed. "Not on your best day!" Michael moved his chair closer to where Jeremy was sitting. "So, how's school?"

Jeremy grimaced at the thought of school. Unlike Michael, he didn't enjoy it. He just wanted to get his diploma and move on. He really hadn't considered college, although his parents had other plans. "You know how it is. Go to school and study, study, and go to school."

Michael had tried many times to help Jeremy get into a better attitude about school, but he had always resisted Michael's efforts. "Jeremy, you'll never get anywhere if you don't go to college. You know that—"

In an effort to change the subject, Jeremy interrupted

Michael. "So, show me what you can do on this new machine, Mr. Linebacker."

Michael knew better than to press the issue. Jeremy was easygoing, but if you pressed him too much he would just make some cute remark and walk out. "I think I've had about all the exercise I can take for one day. Mindy and John, the occupational therapist, about wore me out."

Jeremy leaned back on the machine, placed his hands on the bar and began doing bench presses. Michael laughed at him. "It might help if you'd add some weight to the bar."

Jeremy turned his head, looked at Michael, and smiled. "That's just what I'd expect from a linebacker. The secret is not how much you lift, but how good you look doing it."

Michael threw his head back and laughed. "You're in big trouble then, because you don't look all that great."

Jeremy looked at Michael and sneered. "Jealousy, my man. You're just plain jealous."

"You're hopeless, Jeremy." Michael watched as Jeremy finished his repetitions. "Jeremy! I've got to ask you something kind of serious."

Jeremy stopped what he was doing and gave Michael his full attention. "What's up?"

"You go to church, so I guess you've probably been to one of those Billy Graham Crusades. I was just wondering what they were like."

Jeremy chuckled at Michael's comment. "You may not remember, Michael, but I've told you before that I'm not really all that religious. I go to church, but that's about as far as it goes. I've never even watched him on TV. Why in the world would you ask me that?"

Michael began to feel a little uneasy. He never felt comfortable talking about religion, especially when he was talking to his buddies. "Kelly asked me to go with her next week. I was just wondering what they were like."

"I can't help you, buddy. Sorry!"

Michael smiled, and quickly changed the subject to something they both knew very well. "You hungry?"

Jeremy jumped off of the machine and headed for the doorway. He stopped and looked back at Michael. "You coming?"

Michael laughed, shook his head, and they both headed toward the kitchen.

■ ■ ■ ■ ■ ■ ■

Michael was sitting in the living room alone. Jeremy had left after he and Michael had eaten their fill of chocolate chip cookies. He was thinking about Kelly's invitation. He knew what his mom had said was true. Sometimes, you had to put the feelings of someone you care for before your own. Still, in spite of Kelly's assurance, he felt uneasy about going to the crusade. He wondered if his dad had ever had to do something his mom wanted him to do when he didn't want to.

He looked at his image in the mirror that hung on the living room wall. "You're a coward, Michael Fredricks." He smiled. Jeremy was right—he had flipped out. Now he was talking to himself in the mirror. Michael shook his head. *You're really making it hard on me, Kelly.* Michael took in a deep breath and let out a long sigh.

He picked up the phone and dialed Kelly's number. The line was busy. "Maybe that's a sign," he thought. "I'm not supposed to go."   Michael hung up the phone and it rang. He looked at the phone as if it were possessed. "Hello?"

"Hi! Michael! It's Kelly. I was wondering if you've decided about going with me to the Billy Graham Crusade."

Michael laughed. "This is too weird. I just hung up the phone from trying to call you."

Michael could hear the hesitation in her voice as she asked, "So, are you going to go?"

"Yes! I'll go with you." Michael spoke the words, but still wasn't certain he had made the right decision. He only knew that she wanted him there, and that was enough for him.

CHAPTER 10

The smell of breakfast cooking drifted into Michael's room. He rolled over and smiled. He always looked forward to the weekend when he could enjoy the big breakfast his mom would cook for him. He could hear her singing in the kitchen. She worked hard all week and said she looked forward to taking her time cooking breakfast on Saturday. Michael knew that when it was ready she would walk into his room and softly awaken him. He was usually awake before she came in, but he knew that she enjoyed the ritual, so he would fake being asleep.

Michael was lying on his bed listening to his mom, when he suddenly realized what day it was. It was the day he was supposed to go to the Billy Graham Crusade with Kelly and her family. Suddenly, the aroma from the kitchen was overshadowed by the thought of going to something that was completely foreign to him.

Kelly had reassured him that he would enjoy it, but he was far from certain that she was right. Why should he enjoy it when Jeremy, who went to church, wasn't going?

He wondered if it was too late to cancel out. He could call her and tell her he was sick. He knew she would understand. He felt guilty for even thinking about lying to Kelly. Michael's dad had always encouraged him to be truthful to everyone, especially someone he cared for. He had seen his dad be faithful to that belief many times— even when it might not have been what that person wanted to hear. Michael's mom had said more than once that his dad's truthfulness was one reason their marriage was so strong. She knew she could always trust him.

He was still thinking about his situation when he heard his mom softly calling his name. He grinned as he heard her. She always sounded as if she were calling to a five year old.

"Michael! Michael, honey. Are you awake?"

Michael rolled over and stretched, as if she had just awakened him. He looked at his mom and smiled. "I'm awake. Something sure smells good."

"If you want to get up, your breakfast is ready."

He loved to tease his mom and would take every opportunity to do so. "It smells good, but I'm not very hungry. I think I'll just sleep in this morning."

He could hear the disappointment in her voice. "That's okay. I'll just—" Without warning, his mom ran across the room and jumped onto his bed. She knew how he hated to be tickled, so she gave him the best tickle she could manage. "Do you think for one minute that I don't know when you're asleep, and when you're not? You're not fooling me, young man."

Michael was laughing and yelling for his mom to stop. He told her if she didn't stop he was going to wet the bed.

She laughed, and told him she would just let him lie in it. Mary stopped her harassment and sat on the edge of the bed. "Just remember one thing. A mom always knows when her child is faking something. That's what makes us moms."

Michael laughed and tried to push his mom out of bed. "You get crazier every day. Don't you know it's not nice to pick on someone who has been injured?" Michael was kidding, but he saw the pained look on his mom's face. It was as if she had forgotten, for a moment, that he was injured. He was sorry for the remark, but in one brief moment, the atmosphere had gone from a happy one, to a serious one. "Hey! Mom. I was just kidding. Don't be so glum. I'm going to be alright. I promise."

Mary smiled at Michael's remark. She knew that deep down he wasn't completely convinced that he was. Just like she had told him, *There are some things a mom just knows.*

She placed her hand on his and looked deep into his eyes. "I really hope that you can keep that promise."

Michael wanted to get her back into a lighter mood so he said, "Hey! Enough of this gloom and doom. I'm hungry, and if we don't get out of here my breakfast will be cold."

Mary stood to her feet and looked at him. "It would serve you right for trying to fool your mother."

She turned to leave when Michael stopped her. "Mom! Could I ask you something?"

Mary stopped and faced him. She knew from the

sound of his voice that it was a question that deeply troubled him. "Sure! What is it?"

"I'm kind of sorry that I told Kelly I would go with her today. I don't want to disappoint her, but I'm just not sure what I've gotten myself into."

"Michael, there's something I've never shared with you. I don't know why. Maybe I was afraid that you wouldn't understand. When your dad was sick, a friend of mine asked me to go to a revival meeting with her. She told me that there would be a lot of people there who could pray for your father. She kept trying, but I made all sorts of excuses not to go. There have been a lot of times when I have thought that maybe I should have gone. My reluctance may have cheated your dad out of a chance to live. I don't know. Although you and I may not understand why Kelly asked you to this crusade, it must be important to her. I can't make the decision for you. You made the commitment; you have to be the one who decides if you want to keep it."

Michael knew that she was right, but he had hoped she would give him a better answer than that. One like, "Don't go." He smiled ruefully at his mom and said, "Thanks a lot!"

Mary smiled, turned, and walked out of the room. He lay there locked in his thoughts. He knew that he didn't want to disappoint Kelly. Reluctantly, he decided that he would go, but he decided not to give in to Kelly so easily the next time she asked him to do something. He heard his mom calling from the kitchen.

"I thought you were hungry!"

Michael smiled and shook his head. "I'm coming!" He threw off the covers and grabbed the bar above his bed. He hated all of the apparatus hanging around the house. He knew that he couldn't maneuver without them, but they were just one more reminder of the situation he was trapped in. Silently, he vowed to personally take down every one of them when he was walking again.

Michael was waiting on the porch when Kelly and her family pulled into the driveway. He watched her as she got out of the van and walked toward him. She looked beautiful.

She was wearing a dress that made her look very feminine. She always carried herself well, but she seemed even more graceful in a dress. Michael had never seen her in one, but he liked what he saw. "You look great!"

Kelly smiled at him. Michael noticed the little dimples that formed when she smiled. She hated them, but he told her he thought they were cute. She walked up the ramp and onto the porch. "Are you ready to go?"

Michael could feel the apprehension start to take over again, but he had made the commitment, and he was going. Besides, how bad could it be? He was going to be there with the prettiest girl of all. "Sure! Let's go."

Kelly's dad had the door to the van open by the time she and Michael got there. He helped Michael into the van and stored his wheelchair in the back.

Steve Carlisle pulled the van onto the highway and headed for Columbus. The first few miles were driven in silence. Michael wasn't sure what to say. He had never been around Kelly's dad and mom much. He felt more than a little awkward. He had no idea what to talk about. What could they have in common? As if sensing his thoughts, Steve said, "Michael, are you a Reds fan, or an Indians fan?"

Michael was surprised to learn that Kelly's dad was a sports fan. He thought since he didn't have a son that he wouldn't be interested in sports. "Actually, neither. I like the Dodgers."

Steve laughed. "I guess I thought all Ohio boys liked at least one of the Ohio teams."

Michael could sense the gentle spirit of Kelly's dad. He began to relax, and they spent the next hour discussing every sport they could think of. Kelly and her mom carried on their own conversation, knowing all too well how much men loved to talk about sports.

Before Michael realized it, they were reaching their destination. He looked out the window of the van and could see the stadium. The familiar horseshoe-shaped stadium stood out clearly. Kelly looked at Michael. She could see that he was staring at the stadium. "Would you like to play there, Michael?"

He smiled broadly. "Who wouldn't?" Kelly felt bad for saying something like that to Michael. She hoped that it hadn't bothered him. She didn't want to make him feel worse than he already did about not being able to walk. Thankfully, she could see that he was too interested in what was going on outside the window to have thought about what she had asked.

Michael noticed that the closer they got to the stadium

the heavier the traffic became. "Is the traffic always this bad here?"

Steve smiled. "Not really, Michael. Most of these people are here for the crusade."

Michael couldn't believe his eyes. The traffic was lined up for what seemed like miles. There were policemen and deputy sheriffs everywhere. "I never dreamed there would be so many people. Is it always like this at one of these things?"

Kelly smiled. She was enjoying Michael's surprise. "His crusades are always this crowded. He really is very popular."

Michael watched in awe as throngs of people walked toward the stadium. He wondered how Kelly's dad kept from getting frustrated with all of the stopping and starting.

Finally they reached the parking area. One man, noticing the wheelchair in the back of the van, motioned for Steve to go a different direction. He followed the man's lead and was soon headed for a spot closer to the stadium. They were ushered into the handicapped area. Steve looked in the mirror at Michael. He was trying to see Michael's reaction to being placed in the handicapped spot. Steve's fear was quickly relieved as he heard him say, "We must be privileged people."

Steve agreed. "We are indeed privileged, Michael."

Steve parked the van, took out Michael's wheelchair, and helped him into it. They headed for the entrance and again were directed to a different area. Michael and Kelly's family were ushered to a spot on the field in front of the platform. After they had taken their seats, Michael whispered to Kelly, "Aren't you glad you came here with me? Look at these great seats I got you."

Kelly fought back a tear of joy and relief. "Yes, Michael. I'm very glad I came with you."

Michael sat silently. He was watching everything that was going on. He was amazed at the size of the platform and couldn't believe the amount of equipment positioned around the field. Television cameras, soundboards, speakers. He felt more like he was getting ready for a great concert instead of a church meeting. He looked at Kelly. "This is incredible! I can't believe they've got all of this stuff here. Is this going to be on television today?"

Kelly explained to him that they would tape the program and show it later. She hadn't known that either, until she had asked her dad the same question.

Michael was still busy trying to take everything in when he heard someone say, "Good afternoon! I would like to thank you all for coming here this afternoon."

Michael looked at Kelly. "Is that Billy Graham?"

Kelly smiled. "No! That's Mr. Barrows. He works with Mr. Graham."

Kelly's mom heard Michael's question and told him that Cliff Barrows was in charge of leading the singing. Michael sat back in his chair and watched as the entire crowd started singing a song that sounded foreign to him. He was amazed at the way the sound carried in that huge stadium. He looked around at Kelly and her family who had joined into the singing. Michael was surprised when he heard Kelly sing. She had a very good voice, and even though he didn't know the song, he enjoyed hearing her sing it.

Michael sat motionless in his chair. He began to feel a lot better about being there. He looked down the rows beside and in back of him and noticed that there were a lot of people in wheelchairs. He nudged Kelly. "Are there always this many people in wheelchairs at these things?"

Kelly looked around. "I don't know. I've only been once before, and we didn't get to sit this close."

Michael listened as Cliff Barrows announced that he would like to welcome a very special guest. "Would you please help me welcome Mrs. Joni Erikson-Tada?"

Michael heard the great round of applause. He looked at Kelly, who looked about as bewildered as he was. "Who is she?"

They were both stunned as Joni, in her wheelchair, took her place at the front of the platform. They looked at each other as Michael asked, "Did you know she was going to be here?"

"I didn't recognize her name. I've heard of her, but I guess it didn't register who she was."

Michael looked at Kelly as if he wasn't totally convinced that she didn't know what was going on all along.

He listened as Joni shared her testimony. When she shared that she had been hurt in a swimming accident, Michael looked at Kelly as if to say, "Like this is all a coincidence."

Kelly shrugged her shoulders.

He was amazed when she showed some of the paintings she had created using her mouth. He listened as she concluded her talk with a song. She had a beautiful voice, and Michael was caught up in the emotion and power with which she sang.

The audience gave her a standing ovation as she left the stage. Michael stared straight ahead, as he thought of all of the things Joni had said.

Kelly looked over at Michael, fearful that he was upset by Joni's testimony. She was afraid he might think that she brought him so he could see that being in a wheelchair wasn't the end of the world. Michael turned his head and looked deep into Kelly's eyes. He didn't say anything, but she could tell that he was bothered by something. *How could I have been so stupid?* she thought. *He may think I don't believe that he's going to get better.*

George Beverly Shea was introduced, and when he had finished singing, Billy Graham came to the podium. Michael listened intently as Mr. Graham shared his message. He had never heard anyone talk about God the way he did. It was as if he knew Him personally, which Michael knew wasn't possible. Still, Mr. Graham said some things that made him think. Before he knew it, the message was over, and Mr. Graham was giving an invitation for anyone who wanted to know Christ personally to come forward.

Kelly was watching Michael. She was trying to get inside his head. She wanted to know what he was thinking. What did he think of the service, of what was taking place now? Her heart was racing as she began to pray. "Oh God! You know that I was innocent about knowing Joni was here. I don't want Michael to think I don't have any faith in his recovery. I don't know what he's thinking, but you do. Please, if it's your will, let him go forward. Let him see how much you love him."

Michael couldn't believe the number of people who were pouring onto the field. Young and old alike were taking their place in front of the stage where Billy Graham was standing with his head bowed. Michael could sense that something special was happening all around him. He felt a warmth inside of him that he had never felt before. He could hear people crying as they made their way to the huge stage.

Kelly's heart was pounding as she watched for Michael's reaction. She kept praying that, somehow, something that was said tonight would have had a positive impact on Michael. She was ready to go with him if he would just say the word.

Michael turned his head and locked eyes with Kelly. She held her breath.

"I'm glad I came. It wasn't anything like I thought it would be."

Kelly's heart sank as she realized that Michael was not going to make the commitment she had hoped for. She tried to cover up her disappointment but knew she wasn't doing a very good job. "I'm glad! I really didn't know that Joni was going to be here."

Michael smiled. "That's okay! I enjoyed listening to her. One thing did bother me. I've heard a lot of people talk about the healing God has done in different lives. Why would someone like Joni not be healed?"

"I wish I could answer that question, but I can't. I

don't know why God heals some but not others. I guess He just does. Pretty lame answer, huh?"

Before Michael could answer her, Kelly's mom told them that they needed to leave. She said Steve wanted to try to beat some of the traffic.

The trip back to the van was simple enough, but it seemed as though everyone had the same desire. Traffic had already backed up, and everyone was trying desperately to juggle for position. Michael watched as Mr. Carlisle skillfully maneuvered the van through the maze of traffic. What was even more amazing was the fact that he did it without losing his cool. It wasn't long before they were out of the heavy traffic and on their way home.

Michael took one last look at the O.S.U. Stadium. He could still see the huge line of cars and buses that were still jammed into the parking lot. He shook his head and smiled. "I'll bet some of those people will be there for a long time."

Steve glanced at Michael in the rearview mirror. "Now you can see why I like to get out of there as soon as possible."

Kelly's mom turned around in her seat and faced Michael. Hesitantly, she asked, "So, what did you think of the service?"

Michael could sense that she was asking the question with a little bit of apprehension. "I enjoyed it. I didn't think I would, but most of it was pretty interesting. There is one thing that I don't understand. If God can do all of the things that Mr. Graham talked about, why doesn't he heal someone like the lady in the wheelchair?"

Connie shook her head and smiled. "I really don't know the answer to that, Michael. People must ask that question a hundred times a day. Every time a loved one dies or is injured in an accident, someone wants to know why. I try to remember that God has a special plan for each one of us. For some, it's one grand thing after another. For others, it's one heartache after another. I can't tell you what determines the outcome of a person's life, but I can tell you who. I guess I'm one of those who has been blessed with a simple mind. I don't try to understand why everything happens the way it does. I leave that to those men and women who study for years to solve those mysteries. I just trust God to keep His promise never to leave or forsake me." Connie shrugged her shoulders and smiled. "I know that probably doesn't help much, but it's the way I try to look at it."

Michael smiled. "I think you and your daughter think an awful lot alike."

Connie looked at Kelly and smiled affectionately. "I'm glad you think so. I consider that to be a great compliment."

Steve didn't want the trip home to be a solemn one, so he said the one thing that was certain to turn the conversation around. "Who's hungry?"

He had said the magic words, and soon everyone was offering suggestions as to where they should eat. The sun was beginning to set when the van pulled into Michael's driveway. Mary was sitting on the porch. Steve got Michael's wheelchair out of the van and helped him into it. Michael thanked Kelly for inviting him and said goodbye to her and her mom. While Steve went with Michael to help him up the ramp, Kelly was lost in her own thoughts. She had looked forward to this day, and now it was over. The crusade was just a memory. Her prayers for Michael seemed to go unanswered. She closed her eyes. "Father! I did all I could. I guess the rest is up to you."

CHAPTER 11

Michael awoke to the sound of rain. The air coming through his window felt cool. The breeze was a welcome relief from the record-high temperatures of the last few weeks. He turned to watch the rain as it left a trail down his window. He could hear the birds singing as if they too were enjoying the change. In the distance he could hear the sound of a car driving through the wet streets.

Michael began to think about how much more he was beginning to appreciate the little things in life. Things he had always taken for granted. Things like the sound of rain, or the colors of the evening sky as the sun set beyond the horizon. Even the many things his mom had always done for him took on new meaning, especially since he had become so dependent on her for what he used to do himself. *But all of that is beginning to change,* he thought. He could feel that he was gaining strength, and he was slowly beginning to be able to do more for himself.

His thoughts turned to the message he had heard Mr. Graham give the day before and the stirring testimony of Joni. She seemed to be so content with who she was and her circumstances. One thing still bothered him: he wondered why, if she believed in God so much, He had let this happen to her? She talked about her faith in God; surely He could heal her. He remembered all of the times Kelly and Mindy had told him about the healing power of God. Why would he leave someone who seemed as nice as Joni in a wheelchair?

The sound of the front door closing broke his concentration. He looked at the clock and knew that his mom was leaving for work. He felt good about the fact that she no longer had to miss work to care for him. Her company had been very understanding, but he knew she missed the people there. And he was certain that she felt less burdened, although she never complained. He listened as she started her car and pulled out onto the wet highway.

Michael worked his way out of bed as he began the routine that started every day. He knew that his mom would have breakfast ready and waiting for him. Then he would begin the exercises that he felt would get him out of his wheelchair and back into a normal life. He was very thankful to Coach Bryant and all the guys for getting the exercise equipment for him. He knew that his mom could not have afforded to buy it.

Michael smiled as he moved about on his own, feeling very confident about his progress, even though Mindy was still warning him not to get his hopes up too high. "I'll show them all," he whispered. "I'll show them all."

After he finished his breakfast, he rolled into the spare bedroom where he kept his new equipment. He maneuvered his body onto the seat where he could begin a series of exercises that would strengthen his upper body. He knew that, for now, he was dependent on his upper body to keep him going. His legs were still not doing what he had hoped for, but he was determined that they would. He could feel it.

After a few minutes of exercise, he heard the front door bell ring. "Come on in!" he shouted. The door opened and he heard the sound of a familiar and welcome voice.

"It's me, Michael."

"Come on back, Kelly, I'm working out."

Kelly walked in, and Michael's heart was filled with joy. He couldn't get over how close he was getting to Kelly. He was still uncertain about thinking maybe he should let go completely, but he sure enjoyed seeing her.

"Watch out, Arnold. Michael is getting pumped."

"Always the comedian. I think you're spending too much time with Jeremy. I'd better watch you two."

"Good, he's getting jealous. I'm gaining control."

"Dream on! I'm still the master of my own destiny. And I will be back."

"Great! You're even starting to sound like Arnold." They both began to laugh. There was no one else who could make Michael feel as good as Kelly could. She could bring him out of his deepest moments of doubt just by walking into the room. "I'll be done in a few minutes. I just started to work on my upper body."

"That's okay, I'm in no hurry. I'll just check out those bulging biceps of yours."

"Eat your heart out, Arnold." Kelly sat down and began to watch as Michael finished his series of exercises.

"I was wanting to see if you and your mom wanted to ride to graduation with my family."

Michael stopped and looked at Kelly. She could see that the question bothered Michael. He was silent for a moment. "I don't think I'm going to go."

"Why not, Michael? Everyone really wants to see you."

"See what? A guy in a wheelchair? Someone who has to rely on his mom to go the bathroom? I'm not going to go and sit there wondering what everyone is thinking. 'Hey, look at the cripple. Don't you just feel sorry for him?'"

Michael's anger took Kelly by surprise. This wasn't like him.

"I hate this wheelchair, Kelly! I hate being afraid that I'll never walk again. I hate having to depend on my mom for everything. I want to walk again! I want a normal life!"

"Michael, I want all of that for you too, but you can't quit living. It's not fair. Not to you or your mom. Or to me."

"You?"

"Yes, me. I love you, Michael, and I want you to live a normal life, too. But until that happens, you just can't give up on everything."

"You're not the one in this wheelchair, Kelly. You can walk. You can do everything for yourself."

"That's true, Michael, but that could all change overnight. It did for you. There are no guarantees in life.

Don't let your stupid pride keep you from going to our graduation."

Michael looked at Kelly. He suddenly felt sorry for his anger. It wasn't her fault he was in this chair. He realized that she was right—it was pride. But it just hurt too much. Everyone had looked up to him, but now, how could they?

"Well, are you just going to sit there staring at me? Talk to me—please."

"Hey! What's going on in here?"

Michael and Kelly were both startled by Jeremy's voice. They looked up as he walked into the room. "I knocked, but no one answered me. I was afraid something was wrong."

Michael was thankful for his presence, hoping that he could change the subject. "No, everything's okay. Come on in."

"Hi, Kelly."

"Hi, Jeremy. Maybe you could convince Michael that he needs to be at our graduation."

So much for changing the subject, Michael thought.

"What's the big deal? I'll come over and help you."

"That's the point, Jeremy! I don't want your help! I don't want my mom's help! I don't want anyone's help! I want to walk. Can't you understand that?"

Jeremy had never seen Michael like this. He always thought Michael had everything under control. "Chill out, Michael! I didn't come over here to upset you."

"Well, then leave me alone. That's the best way you can help right now."

Kelly had no idea that her proposal would upset Michael so badly. "Michael, I'm sorry I mentioned graduation. I had no idea you felt this way. I thought you were feeling good about your progress."

"I'm just still not to a point where I feel good about facing the kids in school. I want to walk in. I can't do that yet. I'm just not ready. Now, if you can't talk about something else, then just leave me alone. Please. You don't care about how I feel. You don't even really want to know how I feel."

Kelly and Jeremy looked at each other. They felt as if they had just lost their best friend. "Come on, Kelly, Let's get out of here. I guess we're not wanted."

Michael watched as Kelly and Jeremy turned to walk away. Kelly looked back at Michael. She had never felt as sorry for him as she did right now. "You're wrong, Michael. We do care. Too much to see you let your pride keep you from facing reality."

"What do you know about my reality? My reality is this wheelchair. There's nothing you can do to change that."

"Maybe I can't change it, but are you really trying to? Or are you just giving up? Goodbye, Michael."

Michael sat in his chair staring at the empty doorway where his friends had stood. As he heard the door close, he suddenly felt very much alone and ashamed. He rolled himself to the front door and watched as his friends silently got into their cars and pulled away.

He rolled himself back into his exercise room, but it felt cold and lonely without his friends. He looked around the room at the pictures that lined the wall. He'd always kidded his mom about the number of pictures. He'd told her that she was going to have to build another room just for her family pictures. He rolled his chair over closer to the wall, thinking about all the memories contained in those pictures. As his eyes scanned the wall, he saw a picture of him and his dad on one of their fishing trips. He stared at the picture and could almost smell the fresh air near Canada's Rice Lake. That was one of his best memories.

Michael reached for the picture and removed it from the wall. He stared at his dad and felt an overwhelming desire to see him. "Oh, Dad. I need you. Why did you have to go?"

Michael remembered the way his dad fought the disease that took his life. He remembered the way he'd refused to quit. "The devil loves a coward," he would say. "I'm not about to give up on life yet."

Michael looked at the picture for a few more minutes then laid it down. He looked at the walker that Mindy sent home with him. She told him that the walker was his first big step toward being able to walk again. "Once you become stronger, we can get you up on the walker." Her words stuck in his mind and began to encourage him. He looked at the walker and then at the picture of his dad. Moving closer to the walker, he took it in his hands. He locked the wheels on his chair and positioned the walker in front of him. He reached down and moved his feet off the footboards on the wheelchair, placing them firmly on the floor. He gripped the walker until his knuckles turned white from the pressure.

"The devil loves a coward," he said softly.

The muscles in his arms tightened as he began to try to lift himself free of the chair. Beads of perspiration began to break out on his forehead and run into his eyes. His arms began to quiver as he placed more of his weight on them. He could feel himself begin to rise free of the seat.

The determination in his heart was outlined on his face as he struggled to break free of his metal prison. "Come on, body—move!" His legs shook and wavered as he began to try to force them into position. Suddenly his legs locked into position and he stood upright. "I did it! I did it! I'm standing." Tears and sweat filled his eyes, but joy filled his heart. Michael looked at the picture of his dad and smiled as he dropped himself back down into the chair. "Thanks, Dad. I love you."

Michael's heart was racing as he considered all the possibilities facing him now. The doubts and fears seemed to melt away in the hope he now embraced. He was bursting with excitement as he rolled out into the living room to phone his mom. He picked up the phone and began to dial, listening as his mom's line began to ring. "Hello! Mr. Crawford's office. Mary Fredricks speaking."

Michael began to lose control as he heard his mom's voice, and he began to cry. "Michael?"

"Mom! I did it!"

"Did what, Michael?"

"Mom, I stood up with my walker."

Now it was Mary's turn to cry. "You what? When?"

"Just now, Mom. I wanted it real bad, and I did it."

"Michael, that's unbelievable. I wish I'd been there."

"Please hurry home. I want to celebrate."

"I'll be home as soon as I can, honey. Michael?"

"Yes?"

"I love you."

Michael smiled. "I love you too, Mom."

"Does Kelly know yet?"

His mom's words brought back an ugly memory. Why had he been so angry with Kelly and Jeremy? "No, she doesn't."

"She'll be so excited. I'll be home in a little while. Maybe Kelly will help us celebrate."

Michael felt an emptiness in his heart as he hung up the phone. Kelly was the one person, besides his mom, who had always been there for him and he had hurt her.

He stared at the phone for a moment, trying to decide if he should call her. He picked up the phone, began to dial, and then hung up. Crying, he wheeled himself back to his room.

CHAPTER 12

The next few days were filled with a renewed hope for Michael. His mom was busy fixing his breakfast as he lay in bed thinking about how anxious he was to share his news with Mindy. He knew that this was only the beginning, but it was a very good beginning. His thoughts were interrupted by the smell of the bacon and eggs his mom was preparing.

It's funny, he thought, *how much more of an appetite I have since I stood two days ago.*

Michael lay there listening to the sounds coming from the kitchen. His mom was singing. He hadn't heard her sing since before his dad died. It was a beautiful sound. He remembered all of the times his mom had sung to him when he was a child. She even seemed to have a new glow on her face. She'd told him that after his phone call she cried so hard she was afraid someone was going to have to call 911. He hoped that life would start going better for her now. She deserved some happiness.

"Michael! You'd better get up or we'll be late. Your breakfast is ready." Michael rolled himself into the kitchen. "It's about time you got up, sleepy head."

"Good morning to you, too. I just love it when you use those old fogey sayings."

She turned and moved toward Michael with her spatula raised in mock anger. "You'd better watch who you're calling old. Some of us old fogeys still have some spunk left, young man."

"I guess I'd better be careful, or you might just beat me to death with your spatula."

"Have you ever seen what I can do to an egg with this thing?"

Michael smiled. "Sorry, Mom. I guess I just lost my head for a minute."

Mary walked back to the stove and began to prepare Michael's plate. She looked back over her shoulder. "I still can't believe that you stood on your own, and I wasn't here to see it."

"Believe it, Mom! I did, and I wish you had been here. But there's a lot more to come, and you will definitely be involved."

Michael watched as his mom moved about the kitchen. She had warned him many times that this was her domain and he wasn't to mess it up—although she was quick to remind him that the rule did not apply when it was time to do the dishes. "I was lying in bed listening to you sing. It's been a long time since I heard that."

She turned and leaned back against the counter and looked at Michael, pausing for a moment. Then, with a tear forming in her eye, she said, "It's been a long time since I felt like singing."

"I hope you're going to be doing a lot more singing real soon."

"I hope so too, Michael."

"Mom, Could I ask you something?"

"Sure, honey, what is it?"

"Do you believe in God?"

Mary looked at Michael and then walked over and sat down beside him at the table. "The Billy Graham Crusade must have stirred up something inside of you."

"It was pretty cool, even though I didn't understand a lot of it. I really liked Joni."

"The girl in the wheelchair?"

"Yeah! Even though she won't ever walk again, she didn't seem to mind. She said she wished that she could, but if God said 'No,' she could accept it. I've just never heard you talk about God much, so I wondered if you believed in Him."

She folded her arms and stared straight ahead. Michael saw a look on his mom's face that he had never seen before.

"There was a time, Michael, when I was very close to God. When I was a little girl I was raised in a Christian home. Your grandma, my mom, was a very good Christian. Unfortunately, she died when I was sixteen. I became very bitter toward God and quit going to church. Dad was a very busy man, and he never pushed the issue, so I just drifted away from God."

"How do you feel about Him now?"

Mary looked at Michael. "I really don't know, but I do know one thing."

"What's that?"

"I have been talking to Him a lot since your accident. I'm still angry and confused, but when you stood the other day, for the first time in years I thanked God. I don't know, Michael, maybe—just maybe—something good will come from all of this. When you called and told me your good news, Mom's favorite scripture verse came to me: Romans 8:28. 'All things work together for good for those who love the Lord, and are called according to his purpose.' She believed that with all her heart. Maybe somewhere, somehow, she knows what's going on."

"You never told me that Grandma was religious."

Mary smiled. "Mom would always correct me if I said that she was religious. She would always say that she was not religious, she was a Christian."

"I wish I could have known her."

"I do too, honey. I wish she were here right now. I just know that somehow she could make things better."

"Do you still miss her?"

Michael saw a glow on his mom's face that seemed to fill the whole room. "I miss her as much now as the day I first lost her. She was my best friend." She looked at Michael. "A lot like you and your dad."

Michael smiled. "Then I know how much you miss her. I think about Dad almost every day."

"I do too, Michael." They exchanged looks that transcended any known language. One heart to another. That moment seemed to mark the beginning of an even deeper relationship between Michael and his mom.

Mary spoke first. "We'd better get going, or we're going to be late."

Michael turned and wheeled himself out of the kitchen.

"Michael, you didn't even eat your breakfast!"

She could hear his voice from the other room. "I'm not that hungry. I can't wait to see Mindy and show her what I can do."

Mary began to clear off the table but stopped and sat down. She folded her hands and lifted her eyes toward heaven. "God, I don't know if you will still listen to me. But my son is very excited that he could stand the other day. So am I, but I know he has a long way to go. Please, if you can hear me, don't let him be hurt again. Please."

Mary felt a warm glow fill her heart and a smile lit her face. "Thank you, God. Somehow I know you heard me."

She got up and finished her chores, humming a song she hadn't thought about for years.

■ ■ ■ ■ ■ ■ ■ ■

Mindy Thomas was busy putting away some of the equipment she had been using when she heard the voice of a very excited young man. "Mindy! Guess what?"

She turned and saw Michael wheeling himself into the room, his face glowing, grinning from ear to ear. "What in the world is it, Michael?"

Michael stopped his chair right in front of Mindy. He looked at her and blurted out his news. "I stood the other day, Mindy! I was kind of angry, and I just made up my mind that I was going to do it, and I did."

Mindy knew that Michael was determined to walk. But she also knew, as a professional, that this was only the beginning, and she didn't want to get his hopes up too high.

"Michael, that's great! But we still have a long way to go. A lot of hard work ahead of us."

"I know that! But I'm more convinced than ever that I can do it."

"Then let's get to it."

Mary watched from the doorway as Mindy wheeled Michael to the exercise bars. She was thankful that Michael had such a good relationship with Mindy. She knew that there was something special about her. She watched for a few minutes and then walked away.

Mindy moved Michael to the bar. "Think you can do it again?"

He looked at her and then at the bars. He looked back at her and smiled. "Yeah, I sure do."

She positioned him next to the bars, before stepping away. He looked at her. "I could use some help here."

Mindy smiled. "No can do. You said you stood; so do it."

"Are you serious? These bars are higher than my walker."

"You're going to face a lot of obstacles down the road. Show me how much you want to walk."

Michael placed his hands on the worn wooden bars. Then he looked at Mindy. His heart raced as he tightened his grip. He thought of all the other hands that had held these bars, and wondered if they had been as frightened as he was. He looked at Mindy again.

"Go ahead, Michael. Go for it."

He smiled and stared straight ahead. He began to flex his arms and tighten his grip. He could feel himself rising slowly off the chair. His heart was racing; his palms were sweating. He tightened his grip again and pushed up the final few inches. His voice filled the room. "I did it Mindy! I'm standing on my own again. I want to take a step."

"I don't know if you're ready to do that, Michael."

"Please! Before I lose my nerve or strength."

Mindy motioned for another therapist to come over. "Jim, would you give me a hand? This young man wants to walk."

Jim stood beside Michael. Mindy looked at him, her smile giving Michael even more confidence. "Go ahead. Prove the doctors wrong."

Michael looked at Mindy and Jim. "Go ahead, son. You can do it. I'll be here for you."

Michael felt every fiber in his body tense as he struggled to make his legs move. The struggle moved him to the edge of exhaustion. He felt the pain of the stress in his back. Suddenly he felt his right leg begin to move forward. He was straining so hard he was certain he was going to pass out. Finally he succeeded. The leg slid under him and he locked it in place. He continued the struggle with his left leg and slowly moved it into position beside the right one. Mindy moved the chair under him, and he dropped into it. He looked at her and laughed so hard everyone in the room stopped and watched him.

"I did it, Mindy! I took a step!"

Mindy rolled Michael back away from the bars and threw her arms around his neck. "Way to go, Michael." She stood up and looked at him, wiping her own tears from her eyes. "You just made medical history. Normally someone with an injury like yours doesn't make this kind of progress this fast—if at all."

"I knew I could do it! I just knew I could!"

Michael was so excited that he hadn't heard the applause that filled the room. Everyone was smiling and cheering for him. He felt a little embarrassed, but very, very happy.

"What in the world is going on in here?"

Mindy looked up and saw Michael's mom standing in the doorway. Mary looked at Mindy, a tear in her eye. "No! Don't tell me he stood again, and I wasn't here?"

"Not only did he stand, Mary, he took a very big step."

Michael looked at his mom. His face was beaming, his hair wet from perspiration—a testimony to his effort. "I did it, Mom! I wish you had been here, but I did it."

Mary ran across the room and threw her arms around his neck. "It's not important. The important thing is that you're making progress. You're going to walk!"

"Excuse me. I don't want to be a wet blanket here, but we are not home yet. He still has a very long way to go."

Mary stood up and looked at Mindy. Gratitude filled

her face. "I know that! But I never really was convinced he would get this far. I'm very grateful to you."

"Give Michael a lot of the credit. He is one special young man. I rarely see his kind of commitment and faith, even in men a lot older than he is."

"Don't forget to thank God."

Mindy and Mary, startled, looked at Michael. "What did you say?"

"Mom, I'm still not convinced about how I feel about God. But you did say that you had been praying. Didn't you?"

"Yes, I have."

"Well, maybe He's listening to you."

Mary remembered her prayer at the kitchen table. She felt the same glow that she felt then, and she issued a silent "thank you."

Mindy smiled. "He does listen, Mary. Even when He seems to be a million miles away; He's still listening, and answering."

"Thanks, Mindy. Maybe I'm starting to believe that again, too."

Michael interrupted. "What's next, Mindy?"

"I think you've done enough for one day. You keep exercising those legs because we're about to enter the next stage of your therapy, and you're going to need all the strength you can muster."

"Well, let's get out of here, Mom. I'm hungry."

Mary smiled at Mindy. "Some things never change, do they?"

"I'll see you later, Mindy."

"Okay, Michael. Hey, Michael!"

Michael stopped and looked back at Mindy. "K e e p up the good work."

Michael's smile broadened. "Thanks, Coach, I will."

Mindy watched as he rolled out of sight. She looked at the bar where Michael had taken his step. Fighting to hold back the tears, she issued up her own silent prayer. *God, you never cease to amaze me. Just when I think you can't do more, you prove me wrong. I'm real glad that you do. Thank you.*

CHAPTER 13

Michael sat quietly in the parking lot of his favorite restaurant, waiting for his mom to pay the bill. The sun felt good on his face. He heard children laughing and looked up to see a group of young boys chasing a ball down the sidewalk. He watched as they ran around, each one trying to take the ball away from the other. He smiled, warmed not only by the sun, but also by the thought that maybe one day he too could be running again. Mindy's words of caution only served to strengthen him. He loved to prove her and all of the doctors wrong.

Mary walked out of the door to the restaurant and stopped for a moment. She watched Michael sitting in his wheelchair, her love for him filling her heart. She only wished his dad could see what a fine son he had. She knew he would be as proud as she was. "Hey! Are you going to sit there all day or do you want to go home?"

Michael wheeled himself around. "Would you do me a big favor?"

"Sure! If I can."

"Take me by the school. I want to see if Coach Bryant or Coach Fuller is there. I'd like to see the expression on their faces when I tell them about what happened today."

"Okay. I'll drop you off and run down to the grocery." Mary pulled the car up to the curb in front of the school and stopped. She got out of the car and took Michael's wheelchair out of the trunk. Michael had his door open and was waiting for his mom as she rolled it toward him. "It's kind of funny. We just start to get this routine down and now we may not have to do it much longer."

Mary smiled. "Nothing could make me happier."

Michael maneuvered himself into the chair with ease as Mary closed the door. "I'll be back in about fifteen minutes. Are you sure you'll be alright?"

"Mom, you know I will. I'll be waiting right here for you."

Mary drove off, watching Michael in her rearview mirror. He looked helpless in that chair. She felt the weight of despair start to overwhelm her, but caught herself. "I have to be thankful for all the progress he's made." She smiled as she turned the corner. "You're right, Mindy. He sure is a special young man."

Michael rolled himself down the long sidewalk that led to the football stadium, moving past the gate and out onto the field. He sat there and looked around, letting his mind wander back to the time, just a few short months ago, when these stands were filled with people, and he was on the field. He remembered the day when he intercepted a pass and ran the ball forty yards to score the winning touchdown. He longed to get up and run to the

other end, cross the end zone and spike the football—
something a linebacker didn't get to do much.

"Well, if it isn't the great football star."

Michael turned around and saw Brad Lewis walking
toward him. "Well, I guess some people never change do
they?"

Brad sneered at Michael. "Some of us don't, but I
guess you have."

"What's wrong with you, Brad? What can I possibly
do to you now? Football's over with. We're graduating in
a few days. What's your problem?"

"My problem is that you cheated me out of my last
year as a starter. Before you came, I was the star."

"You're a trip, Brad. You act as if we were playing
professional football. You still got to play. What's the big
deal?" Michael didn't want a really great day to end like
this, so he turned his chair and tried to leave. He started
to move past Brad, but Brad blocked his way. "Brad!
Don't push your luck. I'm just about angry enough to get
out of this chair and kick your butt."

"I don't think a cripple should talk like that. Someone
might just accidentally knock your chair over."

The sneer on Brad's face told Michael that he was
quite capable of just such an act.

"Brad!"

Coach Fuller was walking toward them. The anger on
his face was accented by the veins standing out on his
muscular neck. "What in the world do you think you're
doing?"

"I wasn't doing anything wrong. I was just joking around."

"There's nothing funny about your actions. Now I suggest that you get out of here before I forget that I'm a teacher and that you're a student."

Michael and Coach Fuller watched as Brad walked off the field. Then Coach Fuller turned to Michael. "I'm sorry about that, Michael. I think he has more of a problem than we thought."

"That's okay, Coach. No harm done."

"How are you doing? You look great."

"I feel great. That equipment you guys got me is awesome."

"I can tell you're using it. How's your therapy going?"

"That's what I came to tell you. I walked today. I just took one step, but I did walk."

Coach Fuller gave Michael a high five. "Man, that is terrific news."

"I've got a long way to go, but it's only a matter of time."

"And a lot of hard work."

Michael smiled. "Yeah, a lot of that."

"I hate to run, Michael, but I've got to pick up my wife."

"That's okay. I've got to go, too. Will you tell Coach Bryant for me?"

"You bet I will."

"Tell your wife I said 'hi,' too. She's a nice lady."

"She asks about you all the time, Michael. I'm sure she'll enjoy the great news. Take care, buddy. Once again, I'm sorry about Brad's attitude. I'll see you at the graduation ceremony."

Michael looked at Coach Fuller. In all of the excitement he had almost forgotten about graduation and what had taken place between him and Kelly. The thought cast a dark cloud over the joy of his triumph.

"I'm not—" The words trailed off as Michael thought for a moment.

Coach Fuller looked at Michael. "What's wrong, Michael?"

Michael looked at Coach Fuller and smiled. "You know, Coach, for the first time in a long time, nothing's wrong. I will see you at graduation."

"I'm glad, son. Take care."

Michael watched as Coach Fuller walked away. *You know,* he thought, *maybe being a coach is a great way to stay in football.* Especially if he could be a coach like Mr. Fuller or Mr. Bryant.

Michael saw his mom pull up to the curb. He looked back at the field, took a deep breath, and filed all of the memories away for future use. He turned and made his way down the path to his car and home.

CHAPTER 14

Michael sat in front of the phone staring at it as if it were going to explode. He knew that he had to call Kelly, but he also knew what his last conversation with her had been like. He picked up the receiver and started to dial.

"Michael!"

He slammed the receiver back down in its holder. "Mom, you scared me to death. I forgot you were still home." Michael knew the real reason he was startled was that he was nervous about making this call.

"I just wanted you to know that I'm leaving. I promised Mr. Fletcher down at the market that I would be in today. I'm going to pick up the roast he's saving for me. I won't be gone long. Do you need anything?"

"No! I don't think so."

"Okay! I'll see you later."

Mary turned to leave, and Michael turned back to the phone. "Please be home, Kelly, and please don't still be mad."

He took a deep breath, picked up the receiver, and dialed Kelly's number. He listened as the phone began to ring. His heart was beating so hard he thought it was going to spring right out of his chest. There was a loud click as someone picked up the phone. Michael held his breath.

"Hello?" It was Connie Carlisle, Kelly's mom.

Michael, taken off guard, fumbled for words. "Mrs. Carlisle? This is Michael."

The joy in Connie's voice gave Michael a great deal of relief. "Michael, how are you? Kelly's been hoping that you would call. She was afraid that you wouldn't. Just a minute, I'll go get her."

Michael held his breath as he waited for Kelly to come to the phone. What would he say? How could he apologize for what he had said? He didn't have to wait long, for an anxious young lady picked up the phone.

"Michael! I'm glad you called. How are you?"

Michael felt as if the weight of the whole world had been lifted off of his shoulders. "I'm fine, Kelly. Just a little embarrassed."

"Before you go on, you don't have to apologize for anything. Jeremy and I talked about it, and we knew that you didn't mean what you said. We just thought we'd both wait until you called us."

"Still, it was stupid. You aren't to blame for my accident. I just—"

"If you're going to go on like this, I'm going to hang up." She could tell by the dead silence on the other end of the phone that he didn't understand her comment. "Then I'm going to come over there and shake some sense into you."

Michael laughed and was glad that he hadn't let his pride keep him from calling her. "Thanks, Kelly."

"Now drop the subject and tell me all the good news."

Michael was startled by her comment. Did she know that he had stood by himself? How could she? "What good news?" Michael asked.

"Don't be funny with me, Michael James Fredricks. I know all about what you did the other day."

"How could you know about that?"

"I saw your mom at the store the night of our argument. She told me that you had stood up next to your wheelchair. I told her how upset you were that day. We talked for quite a while about it. She was sure that you would call me, if I just gave you some time."

Michael smiled. He was glad that his mom and Kelly were becoming good friends. She seemed to be growing as fond of her as he was. In a different way, of course. "I hate it when my mom's right."

"We women have our ways, don't we?" Kelly said in a sultry voice.

"I guess that's one of those unsolved mysteries people talk about."

For the first time Kelly felt her fear of Michael's future begin fade away. This first bit of progress was as exciting to her as she was sure it was to him. "You must have been excited. Why didn't you call that night?"

Michael knew that he had been so ashamed of the way he had treated her that he was afraid to call. Now he wished he had. He had been miserable without being able to talk to her. "I guess I was just being stupid."

Kelly laughed. "More of that male ego getting in the way. You guys are all alike."

"Like you women are perfect!" Michael said jokingly.

"Pretty much!" she chided. "Now, please tell me all about what happened."

Michael began to explain to her what had made him decide to try to stand. He told her that he had never felt a greater high than when he felt his legs straighten and begin to support his weight. "You would have thought that I'd just won a big race. Pretty dumb, huh?"

"No, Michael. That's the way I'd expect you to feel. All of the doctors have kept telling you not to hope for too much, too soon. You've proven them wrong. You should be happy about that."

"I am. But it's just like Mindy keeps telling me. I've got a long road ahead of me. I've just got to keep working hard."

Kelly thought about how good it felt to talk to Michael again. She missed his daily calls. She wanted to ask him about going to graduation. She was hoping he had changed his mind, but was afraid to ask. "Michael—"

Michael interrupted her. He wanted so much to make up for the way he had hurt her. "Kelly—" The words were hard for him, because he still felt uneasy about going. "I would like very much to go to graduation with you. That is, if you still want me to."

Kelly's shriek of excitement rang in Michael's ear. "Are you crazy? Of course I want you to go. Your mom and I were already planning for you to join me and my family for dinner afterward."

Michael smiled, more than a little amazed. "How could my mom know that I would go? I've never said anything to her. I was waiting until I talked to you."

"I guess your mom just has a lot of faith in you. She knew you would conquer your fear."

"I guess there are times when she has more faith in me than I do in myself. You two seem to think you have me all figured out, don't you?"

"Just leave everything to us. We'll take real good care of you."

"That's what scares me."

"I thought you men weren't afraid of anything."

Michael chuckled. "Just you women."

"Were you afraid the other day when you stood up?"

"Yes! But I was mad, too. Mad at myself, mad at you, and mad at my wheelchair."

"Your wheelchair?" Kelly asked curiously.

"Yes, my wheelchair. I was mad because I was stuck sitting in it day after day. I had to depend on it to get me everywhere I wanted to go. There are so many obstacles every place I go. Stairs, small bathrooms, small doors, curbs. It gets to me after awhile. The argument we had just made me angry at everything, and I wanted to be in control again. So I just made up my mind and did it."

"See how God works, Michael?"

Kelly's words caught him off guard. "What do you mean?"

"God used your anger for your good."

"That's funny, Kelly. I guess I never thought that God could use people's anger. Does He do stuff like that?"

"I think He does. He knew what it would take to get your attention and motivate you. So He let you get good and angry. I guess He knows you pretty well, doesn't He?"

Michael had never thought about God really knowing him that well. He thought about what Mr. Graham had said about knowing God personally. Maybe this is what he was talking about. "So, God really cares that much about what happens to me?"

"He does, Michael. He's the one who created you in the first place."

"I guess I never thought about it like that. Does He care that much about everyone?"

"Yes He does, Michael. He really does."

Michael still felt uneasy talking about God, so he changed the subject. "Have you talked to Jeremy lately?"

"Yes, he called me last night. He just wishes he could do something to convince you to go to graduation. Are you going to call him, too?"

"No! I want to surprise him. Does he know about my progress?"

"No! Your mom said that we should let you be the one to tell him."

"Man! I'd better watch what I'm thinking around my mom. She knows me a little too well."

Kelly laughed. It was good to hear the confidence in Michael's voice. She couldn't wait to see him Sunday at graduation. "I've got to get off the phone. My dad is expecting an important call. I'm really glad you changed your mind about graduation, Michael."

Michael could feel the love in Kelly's voice, and it warmed his heart. "Me too, Kelly. I'm kind of glad my mom does know me so well. You still may have been angry with me if she hadn't talked to you."

"No way! I'm getting better at understanding you, too. I was just waiting for you to know when the time was right to call."

"Pretty confident, huh?"

"Not really. I just believe God answers prayer."

"My mom and I are finding that out, too. I'll see you Sunday."

Kelly could sense that Michael wanted to say something else, but she didn't want to push him. "Thanks for calling, Michael."

"Sure! See ya." Michael hung up the phone. Sat back in his chair and fought back a tear. He wished that he had the courage to tell Kelly how he really felt about her. He smiled and thought, *Maybe, if she knows me like she says she does, she already knows.*

CHAPTER 15

"Good morning, all you sleepyheads! Time to rise and shine. There's a bright new day just waiting for you! It's seven a.m., and as John Wayne used to say, 'You're burnin' daylight,' and I—"

Michael slapped the snooze button so hard he almost knocked the radio on the floor. He covered his head with his pillow. "That guy needs to get a life. 'Sleepyheads.' He and my mom should get together. They could share old fogey sayings."

"Michael! Rise and shine, you sleepyhead."

Michael smiled. *They definitely need to meet.* "I'm awake, Mom." Michael groaned at the thought of getting out of bed.

Suddenly he realized what day it was, and drew his pillow tighter to his head. "Why did I tell Kelly I'd go to the graduation with her? Man, that was stupid. I'm not ready for that." He rolled over onto his back and lay staring at the ceiling.

Michael could hear his mom singing in the kitchen. He knew that she was excited about his decision to go, although she had insisted that she knew all along that he would.

Michael maneuvered his body out of bed and into his wheelchair. He couldn't get over how much easier the process had become. He was making more progress with each day. His eye focused on a photo of him and his dad that he kept beside the bed. He smiled as he took the photo in his hand, thinking about how anxious his dad had been to see him graduate. He felt a tear begin to form in the corner of his eye and struggled to hold it back.

"Dad! I don't know if you can hear me. I just want you to know that I miss you and wish that you could be here today. I'm trying to take good care of Mom, but it's kind of hard with my injury. But I am getting stronger, Dad, and I know for sure that I'm going to walk again real soon. I wish there was some way you could be there today. I've been thinking a lot more about God, and I wonder if He's there where you are. If he is, Dad, maybe you could ask Him if—if it's okay with Him if you could come today. I don't know if that's possible, but I guess it could be. Seeing as how He's God and all. I miss you, Dad."

Michael set the picture back down on his nightstand, his heart filled with love for his dad. Just as he started to roll his wheelchair into the kitchen, a bright shaft of sunlight shined through the window and onto the picture. The picture seemed to be on fire in the bright light. He followed the shaft of light with his eyes to the window. Slowly he rolled his wheelchair over to the window and opened the drapes completely. Almost as if on cue, a roar of thunder echoed across the dark sky, a sky filled with black ominous clouds. Clouds that, until just moments ago, were unbroken. There, in the midst of the storm, a shaft of sunlight was piercing the clouds and shining its light into Michael's room. He watched as the clouds began to part and the sun broke through, filling his whole room with light. Michael sat motionless, caught up in the beauty of the spectacular sunrise. He looked back at the picture of his father and then turned to go when something outside caught his eye. He looked out the window and saw the most beautiful rainbow that he had ever seen. The rainbow seemed to stretch from one end of the sky to the other. Suddenly his heart seemed to fill with unexplainable warmth and his eyes with tears. "Wow, Dad! I wish you could see this."

"Michael! Come on, honey. Breakfast is ready."

Michael took one more look at the rainbow and wheeled himself out into the kitchen. He didn't know why, but for some reason he felt great, and extremely hungry.

Mary looked up as Michael entered the kitchen and greeted him by throwing the dishtowel at him. Michael feigned pain as the dishtowel hit him in the face. "Ow, Mom! That hurt. Have you been working out again behind my back?"

"Funny boy, you know me better than that. I'll leave all of that physical activity to you. I've got more important things to do."

"You mean old fogey things like knitting or making a quilt?"

"I'll have you know that there are a lot of young people who do those things."

"Oh, I'm sure there are, Mom," Michael chided. "There must be at least—oh, let's say one."

"Laugh if you will, but I'm not as old as you think I am. You're just a young whippersnapper, that's all." Mary smiled, knowing full well that her remark would give Michael a lot of ammunition for future debates.

"'Whippersnapper'? Where in the world did that come from? Next you'll be off playing bingo."

"Well, as a matter of fact, I have been wanting to ask you if you would like to go with me sometime."

Michael laughed. "Me? No way! I'd rather sit down on the corner and watch the traffic light change. But as a matter of fact, I do have someone I'd like you to meet."

"Meet? I don't think so!"

"Sure, Mom! He's got his own radio show. He's a real popular guy with you old fogeys."

Mary laughed. "You'll be sorry someday, when you're old and gray and your children are treating you like you're treating me."

"I've already learned my lesson. No kids! But if I don't get something to eat soon, I may not live to be much older."

"Get over to the table, troublemaker, before I throw it all away."

Michael wheeled himself to the table as Mary finished putting the last of the food in place and sat down. She placed a napkin in her lap and looked at Michael. "Would you mind if I ask a blessing for our food, Michael?"

Michael was surprised but not at all offended. "No, Mom. I think that would be a real good idea."

Mary bowed her head and began a simple but powerful prayer. "Dear God, I know that we don't pay as much attention to you as we should, but we want to thank you for all you have done in our lives. I guess we still have a lot to learn, but we are finding out how very much you love us. Thank you for being with my son. He's very special to me, as I'm sure you know. Be with him today when he graduates. I'm so proud of him for being the valedictorian, and I want him to know that. Please help him in the future as he continues to improve. I guess that's all I have to say, God. Amen!"

Michael looked up at his mom and smiled. "That was great, Mom, except for one small thing."

Mary's expression tickled Michael even more. "What did I forget?"

"You didn't ask a blessing for the food."

Mary looked embarrassed at first, and then they both broke into laughter.

"Way to go, Mom!"

Michael watched his mom as tears of laughter began to roll down her cheeks. Her laughter seemed to light up the whole room. He felt very proud to have a mother like his mother. "Oh, Michael! I guess my first attempt at this was a failure."

"No. I think you did just fine."

When they both settled down, Mary looked at Michael. Her expression changed as she asked, "Are you still worried about getting up in front of everyone?"

"No, not really. I'm pretty cool about it now. I wasn't, but something kind of changed my attitude today."

"Today? You haven't even left the house."

"I know. I can't really explain it. It's just something inside, something I don't even understand yet."

"Well, whatever it is, I'm thankful for it. I didn't want you to do something that would make you uncomfortable. I really am very proud of you."

"I know, Mom. Hey, let's cut all this mushy stuff. I'm hungry!"

"That's my boy!" Mary knew it was time to change the subject. Still, she was very interested in what had happened to put Michael at ease. "I was glad Jeff Peterson called you last night. Did he have fun in Spain?"

"Yeah! He said he did. He said it was sure different from the United States. He's glad he's back."

"How long were they over there?"

"Almost two months. He left just after my accident. He said he wished he could have been here for me. I told him he didn't miss much."

"You didn't tell him how much progress you've made in such a short time?"

"No, I want to surprise him and Jeremy. He's going to meet us at the stadium."

Mary watched as Michael ate his breakfast. She thought about how much he looked like his dad. This was one of those special moments when she missed him more than ever. He would have been so very proud of his son.

Michael finished eating and looked up at his mom. "I love you too, Mom."

Mary looked startled. "What?"

"I knew by the way you were watching me that you were thinking about how much you love me. You're not the only one who knows someone well."

Mary smiled and bowed her head. "Guilty as charged."

"Cut the theatrics, Mom. We've got to get out of here. I'll go get ready while you get stuck with the dishes."

Michael turned and began to wheel himself out of the kitchen. Mary feigned anger as she watched him go. "Now listen here, young man, you get back here right this minute.

I need help with these dishes. I cook; you clean. That's the new deal around here. You're getting better, so now you work."

Michael yelled back over his shoulder. "Nice try, Mom! But you said this is my special day. You wouldn't want to ruin it for me, would you?"

Mary put her hands on her hips. "Men!"

━ ━ ━ ━ ━ ━ ━ ━

Kelly and her parents picked up Michael and his mom at 2:30. The twenty-minute drive to the school was filled with laughter. This was a day Michael and Kelly had looked forward to for twelve years. They could hardly believe it was finally here.

The fear Michael had been experiencing had been

replaced with a great deal of joy and anticipation. He could hardly wait to get to the school.

Steve Carlisle pulled the van up in front of the stadium where a very anxious Jeff Peterson was standing. He left the motor running and moved toward the passenger side of the van. Jeff greeted him and moved closer to the van. Jeff was more than a little nervous about seeing Michael for the first time since his accident. Mr. Carlisle opened the large door on the van and removed Michael's wheelchair. Michael easily maneuvered himself into the chair, rolled the short distance to Jeff, and stuck out his hand. "How's it goin,' Jeff?"

Jeff stood speechless for a moment. Then a tear began to form in the corner of his eye. Michael knew what was happening and moved very quickly to put him at ease. "Hey, Jeff, did they have any Dairy Queens in Spain? I see you still have that manly physique."

Jeff looked at Michael. "I've really missed you. I was afraid you wouldn't come."

"What, and miss a chance to see you trip going up for your diploma? No way!"

"You look great, Michael! You really do."

"What next? Are you going to try to kiss me?"

Jeff looked at him and began to laugh. "You jocks never change, do you? I guess it's in the genes."

"You're just jealous because we get all the girls."

"*Ahem!*"

Michael looked over at Kelly, who was trying her best to look angry. She was standing with her arms folded. "All what girls?"

Michael looked at Kelly and then back at Jeff. "You're back for two minutes and you already got me in trouble."

Kelly moved toward Jeff and gave him a hug. "Good to see you, Jeff."

It was Michael's turn to act jealous. "Just what do you think you're doing, Kelly?"

"I'm hugging my new boyfriend. You seem to have all the other girls in town."

"Cute, Kelly. Real cute."

Mr. Carlisle moved the van to a parking place while Kelly, Michael, and Jeff went in to take their places. The conversation was light between them. It was like old times, at least in some ways. They went to the front of the chairs that were set up on the football field. The field had been covered by a large tarp due to the heavy amounts of rain lately. Still, all things considered, the maintenance crews had done a great job getting everything ready. Mr. Fuller saw the kids and walked over to greet them.

"Michael, it's good to see you. Hi, Kelly! Jeff, I see you made it back from Spain alright. I trust you had a good time."

"Yes, sir. It was great, but I'm glad to be back. I didn't like being away from home for that long."

"I hope you accomplished everything you wanted to."

"I think it'll help me become a better interpreter someday. At least I hope so."

"Good!" Mr. Fuller turned his attention back to Michael. "My wife is anxious to see you, Michael."

"Where is she?"

"She'll be back shortly. Why don't we make our way up to the stage?"

Michael's heart sank. He knew he would be up front, but it was one thing to think about it and quite another to deal with it firsthand. He looked at Kelly and Jeff. Kelly tried to reassure him. "Go on, Michael. You'll be fine."

Michael looked at Mr. Fuller and tried to present the picture of security, while inside he was dying. "Let's go."

Michael looked back over his shoulder as he watched Kelly and Jeff move to take their positions. The ground crew had prepared a ramp for Michael. He had not really thought about how he would get on stage, because he was too busy worrying about being there in the first place. Mr. Fuller pushed Michael up the ramp and moved him into position. Mr. Fuller looked at Michael, seeing the uneasiness in his face.

"You're going to do great, son. I brought your walker like you requested. I'll put it right here beside you."

Michael really liked Mr. Fuller and knew he would be there for him any way he could. "I appreciate everything you and Coach Bryant have done for me, Mr. Fuller. You've both been a great help."

"Your great attitude has helped us too, Michael. You're a special young man, and I'm certain your mom is very proud of you."

"Yeah, she is! Thanks."

"Michael! It's good to see you!"

Michael looked up to see the principal, Mr. Tucker, walking toward him. Mr. Tucker walked up and shook hands with Michael. "You look great, Michael. I'm really glad you could be up here on the platform with us."

Michael felt a little uneasy with the friendliness of the principal. He wasn't used to him showing much attention to anyone. "Thank you, Mr. Tucker."

"We'll be getting started here in just a few minutes. Here's a program for you."

Michael took the program and thanked him.

"I'll call your name when it's time for you to speak."

As Mr. Tucker walked away, Michael thought about what he was going to say. He looked around the audience and could see some of the students talking about him and waving. His heart was in his throat, and his hands were beginning to sweat. He took a deep breath and tried to think of every positive thing he could.

Due to the heavy rains, the usual processional was eliminated. The class was seated in their places and Mr. Tucker walked to the podium.

This is it, Michael thought. *I just want to find a way out of here.*

Michael listened as Mr. Tucker made his opening statements and greeted the guests. He sat there as one by one, they came forward and presented their part in the program. He looked out over the crowd and found his mom sitting with the Carlisles. His heart was beating a mile a minute as his turn to speak drew closer. Finally those dreaded words were spoken.

"Ladies and gentlemen! It gives me great pleasure to introduce to you this year's valedictorian. A young man whose courage on the football field has been matched by his courage to face a serious injury. Will you please welcome Mr. Michael Fredricks?"

Michael moved his walker into place in front of him. He had been placed just a couple of steps behind the podium so he could do what he wanted more than anything to do. He grabbed the walker and pushed himself to his feet. The applause that had started was quickly replaced by a deafening silence. It was as if everyone in the place were holding his breath. Michael struggled to make those two steps to the podium as the crowd watched. Michael had not told anyone, including his mother, about his plans to walk to the podium. He took the final step and stood in front of a crowd that went crazy. In one giant surge the crowd stood to its feet and began to applaud. The thunderous applause was punctuated by the tears on most of the faces.

Michael's heart was filled with joy as he received the respect of the crowd. He watched as they began to take their seats. He took hold of the podium and steadied himself. The crowd grew quiet as Michael began to speak.

"I had a set of notes all prepared for today, but I don't think I'm going to use them. I was afraid to be up here in front of everyone today. I almost lost two of my best friends because of my fear. I wasn't afraid of speaking to you. I was ashamed of the way I would appear to you. I guess I've got a little too much pride for my own good. I look around at all of you here today, and in many ways I envy you. You can walk and run, while I just kind of rock and roll." Michael enjoyed the audience's laughter.

It seemed to put him more at ease. "But I've learned a lot about myself in the last couple of months that maybe I wouldn't have learned otherwise. I think I'm stronger inside, where it really counts. I've grown closer to my mom. I think maybe I even understand her a little better. You mean a lot to me, Mom. Thanks for everything."

Michael looked at his mom, who was busy wiping her eyes, and began to feel tears forming in his own. "I found out that true friends don't leave you just because one day something happens to you and your life's changed. That means a lot to me, guys. Thanks. Mindy Thomas, my physical therapist, helped me find the courage to go on when I really didn't know if I could, or if I even wanted to. She couldn't be here, but I hope she knows what she means to me.

"Two years ago my dad died of cancer. He was my dad, my coach, my hero, and my friend. His death left a big hole in both my mom's life and mine. I wish he knew how many times my thoughts of him have helped me get through the day. Something he may have said, or done, would come to mind, and I found a little more strength to go on." The quiet that filled the stadium was overwhelming. It was as if time had stopped.

"I'll never forget the last thing he said to me. I was sitting on his bed watching him struggle to live. He took my hand and asked me to lean closer so I could hear him." Michael began to struggle to keep from falling apart. "He said he knew that he would miss a lot of things that I would experience in my life. But he wanted me to hold onto the memories that we had shared together. He hoped that from time to time I would find time to think about him and smile. He didn't want me to remember his illness. He wanted me to celebrate his life. He told me he was proud of me. Then he drew his last breath and was gone." Michael reached for the Kleenex that had been placed on the podium and dried his eyes.

"I want to ask all of you not to think about my disability but to help me celebrate all of my possibilities. We may not accomplish all we want to in our lifetime, but we are only limited by our attitude, not our aptitude. Thank you."

Mr. Fuller had moved Michael's chair behind him, and he gratefully dropped into the seat. The crowd rose to its feet. Their applause filled the stadium. Michael rolled back to his place on the platform and breathed a giant sigh of relief. He was shaking like a leaf, but he felt really good.

The final words were spoken to the crowd after the students received their diplomas and the event was closed.

Michael wheeled himself down the ramp where Kelly was waiting for him. She was beaming with pride. "Michael, that was wonderful!" She threw her arms around him. Michael always enjoyed hugging Kelly, but this time was different. He wasn't sure what had changed, but somehow he felt their relationship had moved to a higher plateau.

Kelly kept her arms around Michael's neck and looked into his eyes. He felt something stir deep inside him, as he felt the warmth of her love. He didn't plan it, but in the next instant their lips met, and Michael felt his heart soar. It was a brief kiss, but a special kiss. They looked at each other and, without speaking a word, knew they had sealed the true beginning of a much deeper relationship.

"Hey, guys! Can we join in the celebration?"

Kelly stood up, and Michael felt his face flush. "Sure, Jeremy, why not? Your timing has always been rotten." Jeremy gave Michael one of his ornery looks.

"Don't say it!" Michael warned. "I'm still able to take you on any day."

"Fat chance. You linebackers never could catch us quarterbacks."

Michael searched for the right words to say to Jeremy. He had apologized to Kelly, but not to Jeremy, for the way he had treated them. "Jeremy, I'm really sorry for—"

Jeremy smiled. "I don't know what you're talking about."

"Thanks, Jeremy."

Michael's mom and the Carlisles came up to congratulate the kids. Michael's mom was still drying her eyes. "Thanks a lot, Michael! Now I don't have any makeup left on my face."

Michael smiled. "You don't even need it, Mom."

"He must be hungry. He's being nice to me."

Steve Carlisle grabbed Michael's chair. "Let's go eat."

Michael said goodbye to Jeremy and Jeff. "I guess I'll see you two tomorrow at the picnic."

They both assured him they would be there and moved off to be with their families. Michael saw Mr. Fuller, his wife, and Coach Bryant and asked if he could say goodbye to them. "Sure, Michael."

Mr. Carlisle wheeled him over to them.

Mrs. Fuller was the first to speak. "Michael, you were wonderful. Although I could have done without all the tears. You sure know how to ruin a lady's makeup."

"Thanks! I am sorry about your makeup."

"I'll forgive you this time."

"Michael! I'm sorry I didn't get to talk to you before the ceremony."

"That's okay, Coach Bryant. I was too scared to talk much to anyone."

"You would never know it, son. You sounded as though you spoke to crowds every day."

"Thanks, Coach, but believe me, I hope I never have to do that again."

Michael talked to his coaches for a few more minutes and then said goodbye. Michael turned his chair to leave and then stopped and looked back. "Coach Bryant!"

Coach Bryant walked over to Michael. "Yes, son, what can I do for you?"

Michael paused and looked into his eyes. "Do you remember that job you offered me?"

"The coaching job? You bet I do."

"I was wondering. Is the job still available?"

Coach Bryant looked at Michael and smiled. "You bet it is, Michael. Are you interested?"

Michael smiled. "Yes, sir! I think I would like to give it a try."

"Come on in to my office Monday morning, and we'll talk about it."

Michael's smile broadened. "Thanks a lot, Coach!"

"Thank you, Michael. I asked you to do it because I felt that you could really help our defense. The hours are long, but the benefits are well worth it."

"I'll do my best, sir! Thanks again."

Michael's mind was racing as he thought about all of the possibilities of the job—especially the chance to be involved in football. He wheeled over to join the others, who could tell by the look on his face that something good had happened. Michael saw Brad Lewis watching him but was not about to let him ruin his day, so he ignored him.

Michael joined Kelly, who noticed the glow on his face. "What is it, Michael?" Michael tried to act innocent, but Kelly saw right through him. "Come on, tell me what's going on."

He smiled at Kelly's frustration. "You know what they say about curiosity."

"Michael! You have about two seconds to tell me, and then I'm going to hurt you."

Michael sighed as if he were being forced into telling her. "Well, I guess I don't want you to hurt me, so I'll tell you. Coach Bryant offered me a job, as an assistant coach."

Kelly shrieked with excitement. "Michael, that's great! When can you start?"

"I don't really know yet. I'm getting stronger every day. We're going to talk about it Monday."

Kelly was very proud of Michael. She looked deep into his eyes. "I really love you, Michael."

He looked at Kelly and before he knew it, he said, "I love you too, Kelly."

He began to panic. *What have I done?* he thought. *I can't believe I said that.* His fears were calmed when he saw the tears in Kelly's eyes. Somehow he knew he had done the right thing. Yes, they had definitely moved their relationship to a much higher plane.

He turned his chair around and took one last look at the stadium and his school. "I guess this place won't mean the same thing to us anymore, Kelly."

Kelly looked back at the school and thought of all the great memories. "No, I guess it won't."

They paused for a few moments and then looked at each other and smiled. "Let's go eat!"

As they left the school, Michael's mind was racing with thoughts of what might lie ahead for him and Kelly. Whatever it was, he felt more than ready for the challenge.

CHAPTER 16

Michael awoke to an all-too-familiar sound—the sound of rain falling on his window.

So much for listening to the weatherman, he thought. He placed his hands behind his head and stared at the ceiling in his bedroom. His thoughts went back to his graduation ceremony the day before. He thought about how silly his fears seemed, now that it was over. He was glad that he had taken Coach Bryant's offer of the coaching job. He could still see the surprise on everyone's face when he took his few steps to the podium.

Then his heart warmed, and he began to feel a little flushed as he began to think about the kiss he and Kelly had shared. He couldn't believe that it had happened. *Still,* he thought, *it's not like I planned it. It just sort of happened.* His smile broadened. *I sure did enjoy it!* He wondered if Kelly was upset about it. *She didn't seem to be, but I never could figure girls out. One minute they want you to do something, and the next minute they're mad at you because you did.*

His mind began to race as he thought about the possibilities that could lie ahead for him and Kelly. He was certain of one thing. He knew that he had never felt this way before. He had dated his share of girls, but none of them had ever captured his heart the way she had.

His thoughts were interrupted by the ringing of the phone. He heard his mom talking, but couldn't tell who she was talking to. He heard her say goodbye.

"Who was it, Mom?"

"It was Milly, one of the ladies I work with."

Michael felt disappointed. He had hoped that it was Kelly. His mom walked into the room, her smile telling Michael that she knew he was expecting someone else, and he knew she was about to rub it in. "Were you disappointed, Michael?"

"You think you know me so well, don't you?"

Her big smile made her eyes sparkle, as she enjoyed having the upper hand. "I know you all too well, young man. If you're that anxious to talk to Kelly, maybe you should call her."

Now it was Michael who was smiling like a Cheshire cat. "What makes you so sure I wanted to talk to Kelly? Maybe I wanted to talk to Jeff or Jeremy."

"As you would say, get real! Just admit it. Kelly has stolen your heart."

"I like her, sure. But—"

"No buts about it. You are totally, one hundred percent in love. I saw the way you looked at her last night at the supper table. You're hooked!"

Michael laughed. "What's for breakfast?"

"You can change the subject, but you can't change the facts. She's reeling in the line."

"There you go talking like an old fogey again!"

Michael's mom turned to leave the room but as she did Michael could hear her singing. "Michael and Kelly sittin' in a tree, k-i-s-s-i-n-g."

Michael took his pillow and threw it at her as she left the room. He lay back on his bed and thought about what his mom had said. He knew she was just kidding with him, but she was right. He didn't realize that it was that obvious. He hoped that Jeremy and Jeff hadn't noticed anything. The phone rang again, and his mom answered it. She didn't call him right away so he assumed it wasn't for him.

"Michael! It's Jeremy!"

Michael picked up the phone by his bed. "Hey buddy, what's—"

"Kelly and Michael sitting in a tree, k-i-s-s-i-n-g."

"Mom! I'll get even with you for this." Michael was totally embarrassed. "What do you want, wise guy?"

"How's the love bird this morning?"

"Don't even start, Jeremy! Did you call for a reason or just to torture me?"

"Actually, I had a reason, but this is much more fun."

"Remember, I don't get mad, I just get even." Michael could feel his face flush. "Why did you call?"

"I wanted to tell you what time I would pick you up for the picnic."

Michael saw his chance to have a little fun, so he took advantage of it. "I'm not going to go. I changed my mind."

But much to his dismay Jeremy didn't take the bait.

"No problem. Since you're not going, I'm sure you won't mind if I take Kelly."

"Your time's coming, Jeremy Wethers! I'll remember this. You will be very sorry someday."

Jeremy laughed. "I'll be by about 1:30 to pick you up. Will you be ready?"

"Sure. Just come on in when you get here. Mom has some stuff for the picnic. I'm sure she'll want to congratulate you for doing such a good job harassing me."

"I was going to give you a hard time anyway. She just gave me some good ammunition."

"Is it that obvious how I feel?"

"Kelly and Michael sittin' in a tree—"

"Goodbye, Jeremy!" Michael hung up the phone. He smiled as he thought about his mom putting Jeremy up to a prank. Even though it was more than a little embarrassing, it was great to see his mom so happy again. As he began to make the effort to get up, he paused on the edge of the bed. "But, Mom, I will have to pay you back." He got into his wheelchair and made his way to the kitchen.

Michael rolled into the kitchen and moved to the sink where his mom was standing. "Think you're funny, don't you?"

Her smile was as bright as Michael had ever seen it. "Whatever do you mean? I didn't do anything."

"You know where lying sends you, Mom. If you're saying you didn't do anything, then I think you have a front row seat."

"I meant to say I didn't do anything wrong. I was just having a little fun."

"Whatever, but the wrath of Michael will be upon you two when you least expect it."

"Since you're making statements from the Bible, isn't there something in there about not being angry with someone? Besides, when did you start to talk about biblical things?"

Michael knew his mom was kidding, but he began to feel a little uncomfortable. He quickly rolled to the table and took his usual place. "I've got to eat fast. I need to get some things from town before the picnic. That is, if you'll take me."

Mary was sensitive to Michael's reluctance to talk about religious things. She had trouble expressing her spiritual feelings as well, so she gladly accepted the change of subject. "Sure, honey! I've got to pick up some things I need to finish your share of the picnic lunch."

Michael and his mom quickly finished breakfast, cleaned up the mess, and went into town to run their errands.

True to his word, Jeremy came by at 1:30, loaded Michael into the car, accepted Mary's appreciation for helping her to harass Michael, and drove off. Mary watched as the two drove off, being careful not to watch them drive out of sight. Her mom had always told her that it was bad luck to do so.

Michael enjoyed the short ride to the Riversedge Park where the picnic was being held. He tried to get Jeremy going with a lot of threats of reprisal, but Jeremy was

ronald mccarty

enjoying the game as much as he was. "So when are you two getting married?"

Michael looked at Jeremy who was grinning ear to ear. "Don't start, Jeremy. I'm warning you. I know your weaknesses."

"I will be the best man, won't I? It goes without saying that I am the best man. Linebackers are more animal than man, aren't they?" Jeremy loved to get Michael going.

"Get real, Jeremy! Quarterbacks are all pretty boys. They're too busy worrying about how they look to become a real man."

"You're just jealous because I'm better looking than you."

"In your dreams, Wethers! I've seen better heads on a root beer."

Jeremy laughed. "What kind of a dumb saying was that?"

Michael began to laugh. "Oh no! I've been hanging around my mom way too much. I'm starting to talk like her. I'm becoming my mom."

They both looked at each other and screamed. "Ah!" Their laughter could be heard by everyone in the park as they pulled in. They found a parking place, and as they were pulling in, Jeff and Kelly walked up. Kelly was the first to speak.

"What in the world were you two talking about? We could hear you laughing clear over where we were."

Jeremy helped Michael out of the car and into his chair. Jeremy and Michael spoke in unison. "It's a man thing." They looked at each other and started to laugh again.

Kelly looked at Jeff and said, "It looks like it's going to be a long day." Jeff agreed.

They finished unloading the car and took everything to the spot Kelly and Jeff had secured. It was turning out to be a beautiful day. The rain clouds had moved out, and the sun was drying the grass. The turnout for the picnic was good. Just about everyone was there.

"Michael!"

Michael looked around to see a small group of kids walking toward him.

"We really enjoyed seeing you at the graduation ceremony yesterday."

"That was a great speech."

"Yeah! How in the world did you keep from losing it? It must be tough, being in a wheelchair and all."

The last comment cut through Michael like a knife. That was exactly the kind of statement he didn't need. His reply was more than a little cool. "I'm not brain-dead just because I'm in this chair. I can still function." He saw the look on the faces of those in the group and knew that they hadn't meant any harm. He felt a little ashamed and tried to soothe over his brash comments. "I'm not going to be in this chair much longer. It's just a temporary thing."

"That's great! I guess we'd better get going. See you later." Everyone in the group acknowledged him, and they walked away.

Michael looked at his friends, who seemed a little lost

for words. "Look, I'm sorry. This was exactly the reason I didn't want to come. It's still a little hard to deal with some of the comments people make. I know they just don't know what else to say, but I just don't want their pity."

Jeremy broke the tension. "Hey! Did we come here to have fun or what?"

Jeff spoke up. "I just came for the food."

Kelly, Michael, and Jeremy looked at each other and laughed. "We can always count on Jeff to show up when the food is free," Michael said.

"Hey, for you guys, it's sports. For me, it's food."

Jeremy said, "Speaking of sports, let's go over to the volleyball game."

Michael was a little hesitant, but he agreed to go. He didn't know how he would feel watching from the sidelines.

Jeff said, "I'll catch up with you. I'm going to go get some food."

They all laughed as they watched Jeff head to the food table.

The volleyball game was in full swing when they got there, and it didn't take Jeremy long to get involved. Kelly sat down on the grass beside Michael and watched with him.

"You can play, Kelly. I really don't mind."

"I'm not really in the mood. Would you like to take a walk?"

Michael smiled. "Yeah, that sounds great."

Kelly and Michael walked through the picturesque

park. One by one, the people came up to congratulate Michael on his courage and his speech. He was beginning to feel a little more comfortable about their comments. Soon he began to relax and enjoy the attention.

They went over to the small pond in the center of the park and Kelly sat down on a bench beside Michael. "I've always liked this part of the park the best. I love to listen to the sound of the water flowing from the fountain in the middle of the pond."

Michael looked at Kelly. He could see the joy and contentment on her face. She had never seemed more beautiful to him than she did at this moment. Kelly looked at Michael and smiled. "What are you thinking?"

"Just thinking."

"I'm glad you came today, Michael. I wouldn't have enjoyed it if you hadn't."

Michael wanted to say so much, but he didn't want to say the wrong thing. He struggled trying to find the right words. "Kelly, could I ask you something?"

"Sure, what is it?"

"Were you upset yesterday? When I—I—"

Kelly smiled. Her beautiful eyes sparkled. "Kissed me?"

Michael felt his face flush. "Yeah!"

"I've never wanted anything more, Michael. I would have been very disappointed if you hadn't."

Michael looked deep into her eyes, his love for her filling his heart. He leaned toward her and she responded. His pulse was racing as their lips met. She threw her arms around his neck, and Michael's heart soared. Their kiss was even sweeter to Michael than it was the day before. He felt as though he could jump up out of his chair and run around the park. He sat back, took her hands in his, and said, "I love you, Kelly Carlisle."

Kelly sat down on his lap, threw her arms around his neck, and kissed him. "I love you, too, Michael. Very much."

"I don't know what's going to happen to me down the road, so I can't make you any promises."

"I don't care. We've got our whole lifetime ahead of us. I'm not going anywhere."

Michael felt stronger than he had in years. He looked around, hoping that Jeremy hadn't been a witness to what was taking place. He didn't want to give him any more ammunition.

"Michael, I've got to run home for a few minutes. Do you mind?"

"No, I'll just go back to watch Jeremy play volleyball."

Kelly kissed Michael again and ran toward her car. She turned and smiled at Michael. "I love you, Michael."

Michael watched as she ran out of sight. Quietly, he said, "I love you, too, Kelly."

The game was going full blast when Michael returned. He watched as Jeremy spiked the ball.

"Way to go, hot dog!"

Jeremy looked over and smiled. Michael still didn't feel like watching from the sidelines, so he decided to go down to the river. He could hear the river before he saw it. The heavy rains of the past few weeks had made the river a raging torrent. He rolled his chair up close to the edge and sat in awe at the power of a river that had doubled in size with the abundance of rain.

He was sitting there thinking about all of the things that were happening in his life. For the first time in a long time, he really felt that things were going his way. His thoughts were interrupted by a scream of fear.

He looked toward the source of the yell and saw Brad Lewis hanging from a limb about twenty feet out into the river. He was yelling for someone to help him. "Please! Help me! I can't swim!"

Michael looked around for someone to help him, but there was no one else around. *What can I do?* he thought. *I can't even walk.* His mind raced as he tried to think about what he could do.

"Please! I can't hold on much longer!" The river was swirling around Brad as he clung for his life to the small limb.

Michael noticed that ten feet from shore a little island had formed. The water was shallow there. Maybe there was some way he could get out to it. Michael rolled his chair to the edge of the river. The sound of the rushing water was all he could hear as he worked his way closer.

As he reached the edge, he began to work his chair into the shallow water. It didn't take long for the chair to get stuck in the mud. Michael tried to think of something else he could do. Finally, in a desperate move, he pushed himself out of the chair and tried to cover the remaining distance. Every fiber in his body struggled as he tried to maneuver his legs to reach the edge of the island. The water was less turbulent in the shallow area, and it helped support his weight. Just short of the edge he fell and swallowed a mouthful of water. He struggled to make the final few feet and pulled himself onto the island. He looked around for something to help him. He spotted a small branch that could be long enough for what he had in mind. He grabbed the limb and tried to stand. The struggle had taken most of his energy, and he couldn't stand up, so he crawled to the outside edge of the island.

There was a small tree at the edge of the river that seemed strong enough to support him. He maneuvered his body into the rushing water as he held tightly to the tree and his branch. The hours of working out were paying off as he used his upper body strength to his advantage. He positioned himself so that the end of the branch was sticking out as far is he could reach into the water. He turned his head toward Brad and screamed as loud as he could.

"Brad! Let go of the branch! You should be able to drift right toward me! Then you can grab onto me or the branch in my hand!"

Brad was too afraid to let go. "I can't! I don't want to die!"

"You're not going to! You can make it! It's your only chance!" Michael hoped that he was more convincing to Brad than he felt himself.

Brad struggled against the force of the water. He was beginning to lose his grip. Michael yelled again in desperation. "Come on, Brad! You've got to try!"

Brad looked upstream at Michael, took a deep breath, and let go. The current of the river caught his body and flung him downstream. He felt the tow begin to pull him under. His arms were flailing wildly. Just when he felt that he was already past Michael his hand struck the limb, and somehow he managed to grab it. He clung in desperation.

"Come on, Brad! Use me and the limb to make it to shore!"

Brad slowly worked his way toward the edge of the small island. Michael called on every muscle in his body to hold on. Finally, after what seemed like an eternity, Brad reached Michael and, using his body, pulled himself to shore.

Brad's heart was pounding hard as he lay breathless on the edge of the river. He couldn't believe that he had made it. When he caught his breath enough that he could speak he began to thank Michael.

"I can't believe you thought of that. I can't believe it worked. I don't know what to say. I owe you my life." Brad turned his head toward where Michael had been.

He wasn't there. "Michael?"

Brad began to panic as he realized that Michael was gone. He screamed. "Michael! Oh dear God, no! Michael, where are you?" He began to cry as he stood up and looked down the river. Michael was nowhere in sight. The struggle to save Brad had been too much for him.

Brad collapsed on the edge of the river and began to sob. His sobs were drowned out by the noise of the rushing water. Brad stood up and took one last look down the river. He hung his head and made his way to shore. The weight of the news he had to share tugged at his heart. Slowly he crested the hill and disappeared from sight.

CHAPTER 17

The soft warm breeze blowing through the window caused the delicate lace curtains to flutter noiselessly. Mary, eyes swollen and red from the past two days of crying, lay motionless on her bed staring out the window at the rising sun. She barely had any strength left in her. The events of the past two days seemed like a bad dream. If only it could have been so. She felt as if there were no more tears to cry, no more energy left to keep going. First her precious husband, and now this? *Why?* The question had no answer. There could be no good reason for her son to be taken. Just when things seemed to be turning around for him, he was gone.

She looked at the clock on her nightstand. 6:30. She knew that in seven hours she would be saying goodbye to her son forever. She had requested that the casket remain closed. She felt that it was much better to remember him as he was, full of life, than to have the horrible picture of him in a casket as her last memory of him. She wanted to get up and get started trying to keep busy, but her body would not cooperate. She felt as if her last ounce of energy had been drained.

Somehow she managed to get out of bed. She walked to the window, pulled open the curtains, and watched the beautiful sunrise for a moment. She felt the tears start to roll as she remembered how much Michael had loved the sunrises. He had told her it was like the opening of a curtain on a play. Each time the sun would rise was like another act—full of the promise of excitement and surprises. She wondered if he could see the sunrise.

Mary prepared her bathwater and walked into the kitchen to make coffee. She was standing at the sink filling the coffee pot when she looked outside and saw Michael's bike leaning against the garage wall. He hadn't been able to ride it since his accident, but just a few days ago he had gotten it out. He said he felt as if it would help him to have a goal to ride the bike before summer's end.

Finishing the coffee, she walked back to her room. As she walked past Michael's room, she paused at the door. The door had been closed since the day he died. She looked at it as if any minute he would burst through it and smile. She could hear his laughter, his taunting words, as he would kid her about being an old fogey. Reaching down, she opened the door, walked into the room, and walked over to Michael's bed. The picture of Michael and his dad caught her eye. Picking it up she sat down on the bed and tried to fight back the tears. The reality of Michael's death hit her full force. Mary collapsed on Michael's pillow and, clutching his picture to her chest, mourned as only a mother could for her son.

Mary was startled by the sound of a car door closing

outside. She looked at the clock in Michael's room and saw that it was 9:30. Realizing that she must have fallen asleep, she jumped out of bed and rushed toward the window to see who was there. The days of no sleep and very little food were taking their toll as she nearly passed out from the sudden movement. Regaining her composure, she looked out the window only to find a car that she had never seen before. The doorbell rang, and she felt the urge to ignore it. She wasn't ready to see anyone yet today. The bell rang again. She looked in the mirror and tried to make herself as presentable as possible. The bell rang again and, frustrated, she went into the living room to answer it. When she opened the door she saw a young man that she had never seen before.

"I'm very sorry to bother you this early, but I had to talk to you. My name is Brad Lewis."

At first, the name meant nothing to her.

"I'm the one Michael saved from the river."

Mary's heart froze. She didn't know what to say. All she could think of was, *Why is my son gone and this boy still here?* Wanting to slam the door and scream, she fought back the desire. The young man seemed harmless enough, but what could he possibly want?

"I haven't been able to sleep since that day. Every time I start to fall asleep I dream about that river and how frightened I was. Michael was there, and even though he was limited, he never hesitated to try to do something to help me. I know that I never treated him right, and I know that I can't ask for his forgiveness. But I just wanted you to know how sorry I am for what happened."

Mary stared at the young man for a moment. "I appreciate your stopping here to say what you've said, but what happened was not your fault. My son was a very giving person, and he would have done the same for anyone. You must not have known my son very well, or you would have known that he didn't hold grudges. He never said anything bad about you to me, and we were pretty close. I must admit that it hurts me to see you standing here knowing that in a few hours I must say goodbye to him. But I can't hate you. Maybe it would help me to displace some of the pain and anger, but it wouldn't honor his memory."

Brad looked deep into Mary's eyes as a tear began to form in his. "I really am sorry, ma'am. I wish I could change everything."

"I do too, Brad, but we can't. God must have had some reason for keeping you alive." Mary was surprised at the sound of her own words.

Brad thanked Mary for talking to him and turned to leave. Mary watched as he got into his car and left. She slowly closed the door. Once inside, she began to sob uncontrollably and collapsed onto the floor. She lay there thinking about the final words she had spoken to Brad. *How does God choose one over another to die? Why would one life be more important to Him than another? If He loves us all, why do we have to deal with death at all?* The words sounded empty and harsh to her. She knew that no one but God could answer those questions. Still, they haunted her as she tried to make some sort of sense of Michael's death.

Regaining her composure, she walked off to finish getting ready for one of the worst days of her life.

■ ■ ■ ■ ■ ■ ■ ■

Jeremy pulled his father's van to a stop in front of Kelly's house. She was waiting on the porch. Jeremy's heart went out to her as she sat there staring at him, not knowing what to say. He got out of the van and walked onto the porch.

"Hi, Kelly."

Trying to manage a smile, she greeted him. Jeremy could see the result of two days of crying and the lack of sleep etched deeply into her face. He sat down beside her silently for a few moments. Finally he looked at her. "Are you ready for this?"

Looking straight ahead she murmured, "No." They sat silently and then she looked at Jeremy, tears filling her eyes. "Why, Jeremy? Why did this happen to Michael? Why now? Just when he was starting to get better?" She knew that he didn't have the answer, but she needed to voice the question.

Jeremy looked at her. "I don't know, Kelly. I wish I knew the answer. You're closer to God than I am."

Kelly shrugged her shoulders and looked straight ahead. "It's times like these that I have my doubts about God. If He wanted Brad saved, why did He let Michael die to do it? Why couldn't they both have made it? It's just not fair."

"I wish I could tell you, Kelly, but I can't. I'm sure

Michael's mom is asking the same questions. My dad always says that there are some things we won't understand until we get to heaven. If that's true, maybe Michael's standing in line trying to find out why."

Kelly looked at Jeremy with a questioning gaze on her face. "Jeremy, that's one of the problems. What if Michael didn't make it to heaven? I took him to a Billy Graham Crusade, but he didn't seem to like it much. He didn't make a commitment or anything."

"I don't know how God works, Kelly, and I never talked to Michael about it. I guess I should have, but now it's too late." They both sat silently, then Jeremy told her that they needed to go get Michael's mom. He helped Kelly to the car, and they began a silent ride to Michael's house.

Jeremy pulled the van to a stop in Michael's driveway. They looked at each other and then back at the house. Jeremy drew in a deep breath and let it out with a sigh. "I guess we might as well get this over with." He got out of the van, helped Kelly out, and they walked to the front door. Nervously he rang the bell. They heard movement inside, and then Mary opened the door. They stared silently at one another, and then Mary asked them to come in.

Once inside, Jeremy and Kelly looked around as if seeing the house for the first time. They looked at the pictures of Michael and his family, including his senior picture that his mother had covered with a black scarf. It seemed so unreal that they were there and Michael was not, nor ever would be again. Mary told them that she would be ready in just a few minutes.

Neither Jeremy nor Kelly said a word, but they both knew that they were feeling the same way. The quietness in the house was such a contrast to the way it had always been with Michael around. The memories of all the hours spent here with Michael flooded their minds and warmed their hearts. Soon Mary reappeared, and they loaded into the van and left for the school.

They were anticipating such a great crowd that it had been requested of Mary to have the funeral service at the school. Mary knew that Michael had enjoyed his short time here and felt that he would approve. The parking lot was full as Jeremy pulled up to let Mary and Kelly out. Kelly's dad and mom were waiting for them as they pulled up.

Kelly's dad was the first to speak. He took Mary into his arms and could feel her body tremble as she fought to hold back the tears. "Mary, we are so very sorry. If you need anything at all, please don't hesitate to call us."

"Thank you, Steve. You and your family were very special to Michael. I'll be fine." Mary knew that they were just words, because she would never, ever be fine again.

Kelly and her family escorted Mary to her seat. She had requested that they sit with her, because she had no other living family members. She looked at the casket sitting before her and felt as if she would become sick at any moment. Tears filled her eyes as she looked at the picture that had been placed on top of the casket. Kelly, sensing her despair, reached over and took her hand. They looked at each other in silence. There were no words to express what they were feeling at this moment.

The auditorium was filled with solemn faces. The crowd had been just as large as they had expected. There were even kids there from schools that Michael had played football against, proving the theory that the worth of a life may never be fully measured until it is gone—one more reason to express appreciation to those whose lives enrich ours.

The organ music stopped, and the crowd grew quiet. Coach Bryant had been asked to lead the service and introduce the pastor who would speak.

"Good afternoon. We are gathered here today to say goodbye to someone whose life, although short-lived, touched many of ours. I have never met a young man who was any more compassionate or determined than Michael Fredricks. His short life seemed to be filled with more than his share of heartache, yet I never knew him to be bitter. I'm sure that he had his times of anger and doubt, but he never seemed to let them destroy him. His passing has left more than another opening in my coaching staff. It has left a hole in my heart. He was a very special young man. We have asked one of his good friends to say something." Coach Bryant looked around and motioned to Jeff Peterson. "Come on up, son."

Jeff walked to the podium and looked out upon the crowd. His eyes came to rest on Michael's mom, and he tried to muster a smile. "Mrs. Fredricks asked if Jeremy, Kelly, or myself would say a few words today. I guess I was sort of volunteered by the other two. I don't know what to say, except that Michael was the kind of person who didn't judge people by how they looked. No one paid much attention to me until he became my friend. I never knew why he liked me, but it never seemed to bother him that I was fat or considered a geek. He just let me be myself and helped me to find out who I really was. I'll miss him terribly, Mrs. Fredricks. But I want you to know that he made more of a difference in my life than anyone I have ever met. Thank you for bringing him into my life." Jeff thanked the crowd and took his seat.

Coach Bryant introduced a few others who had asked to say something about Michael. Then he introduced Pastor Bill Sinclair, Kelly and Jeremy's pastor. He walked to the podium and asked everyone to bow their heads in prayer. When he had finished he looked around at the great crowd. He was silent for a moment, and then he spoke. "I never met Michael officially, although we did talk on the phone on one occasion. But I can see by the number of people present here today that he was a very special young man. It's always difficult to conduct the funeral service of a young person, particularly one you have never met. I can't tell you of the warm memories I have of our times together. Nor can I share all of his triumphs and successes, because I did not know him. But his life reminds me of the life of another man whom I have never met, although his life has touched yours and mine greatly.

"He was the son of a simple carpenter, a man of no great physical appeal. A man so full of love and compassion that he was often misunderstood, and mistreated. He was sent to earth to save a world that for the most part would reject him. He too lived a very short time on this earth, but the impact of his life will reach far into eternity.

"Wherever he went, he never left things the same. To some he was Messiah. To others he was a nuisance. Some saw him as someone who could deliver them from their pain and afflictions. But most never really understood who he was until he was gone. In their mourning, he came to his disciples to bring them hope. Their unbelief was soothed by the power of his words and the evidence of the scars on his feet and hands.

"I never met Michael, but I can see the evidence of his impact on the world by the great number of people here today. I also know that what he did so unselfishly was noted in the Holy Word of God. For it is recorded in the fifteenth chapter of the gospel of John, the thirteenth verse, 'greater love has no man than he lay down his life for another.' Michael didn't stop to think of the possible outcome of his actions. He just reacted to the need and went beyond his physical capabilities to save the life of one of his classmates. Please don't ask me why it happened, or why God didn't intervene. I only know this one thing, that no one can ever understand the true heart of God. His ways are not our ways, nor, for the most part, are our ways His.

"I wish that I could leave you with some deep philosophical message of hope. But to be truthful, the message of hope, although great, is quite simple. 'For God so loved the world that he gave his only son so that whoever believes in him should not perish but have everlasting life.' That message of hope is found in John 3:16."

Looking deep into the eyes of Michael's mom, the pastor simply said, "Dear lady, my thoughts and prayers are with you. Although I did not know your son, I have seen the result of his courage. I look around and can see the testimony to his love and compassion in the faces of those present here today. I have a feeling that his effort in saving the life of this young man will not go unrewarded. Perhaps, even as we speak, he is with the other man whom I have never met, but who gave his life for so many. Let us pray."

Coach Bryant closed the service by leading the entire assembly in the school anthem. When they had finished he dismissed them. "Thank you one and all for coming."

One by one, Michael's classmates came up to Michael's mom and expressed their sympathy. Brad Lewis walked up to Kelly and Jeremy, who were standing off to one side of the auditorium. "Can I talk to you for a minute?"

Kelly and Jeremy looked at Brad and back at each other. Jeremy was the first to speak. "There's nothing you can say, Brad. I know it wasn't your fault, but you never had anything good to say about Michael."

"Besides," Kelly said, "it's over. You're still here, and Michael isn't, and that stinks, Brad. That really stinks." The anger in Kelly's voice took Jeremy by surprise. He wasn't used to hearing her speak that way.

Brad hung his head for a moment and then looked at Kelly. "Look, all I wanted to do was say I'm sorry it happened. I also wanted to ask you if I could go to church with you two sometime."

Kelly and Jeremy looked at each other in disbelief. Was this really the obnoxious Brad Lewis they were talking to?

"Why would you want to go to church with us?" Jeremy asked.

"I know you two were good friends of Michael's, and I know that you go to church together. Besides, Jeremy, we are related."

Kelly began to feel herself losing control. She was angry and didn't know who to be angry with, so she began to take it out on Brad. She struck out at Brad with a fury. She wasn't even aware of what she was saying. She was just mad and she needed an outlet. People were beginning to look in her direction.

Her pastor saw the situation and moved in to try to resolve it. He stepped in front of Kelly and began to try to calm her. He turned to Brad. "I'm sorry, young man, perhaps you'd better go."

Brad looked at Kelly and then at Jeremy, hung his head and walked away.

Kelly was shaking hard when her parents arrived. When she saw them she threw herself into her dad's arms and sobbed uncontrollably. "I'm so sorry, Daddy. I just miss him so very much. I just don't understand. It's just not fair."

Mary walked over to Kelly, reached out and touched her cheek. Kelly looked at her. "I'm so sorry, Mrs.

Fredricks. I wanted to be strong for you. I'm sorry I let you down."

Mary looked at her with love. Kelly could tell she understood. "It's okay, Kelly. It's okay."

Kelly tried to regain her composure. She looked at Jeremy. "I guess I kind of blew it, huh? Real good Christian attitude."

Jeremy smiled at her. "You just said some of the things I wanted to say. None of us really know what to do or say, Kelly. It's real tough to lose someone."

Steve Carlisle looked at Mary. "Why don't we take you home, Mary? We'll let Kelly and Jeremy talk to some of their friends."

Mary smiled. "That would be fine. I've got a lot of food to get ready. Some of the church people brought food. I hope you'll stay and have something to eat."

Connie Carlisle assured her that they would stay. Mary looked at Kelly. "My son really found a winner when he found you, dear. He loved you very much. Stop by later if you can. If you don't, I'll understand. Just don't lose touch, okay?"

Kelly smiled. "You know I won't lose touch. Thanks."

Mary said her goodbyes to those who were standing by and walked away. Kelly could see the deep despair in her heart by the way she carried her body. She wished that there were some way she could help. But she knew that only time and God could comfort her. For now she had only the memories.

Kelly watched as Mary walked out of the auditorium. She looked at Jeremy and watched as Michael's casket was wheeled out. At Mary's request there was to be no graveside service. She felt that it would be too much for everyone. Besides, he had told her that it was too hard to deal with when she had buried his dad.

Kelly looked at Jeremy. "Could we take a ride? I just don't feel like being around a lot of people right now."

"Sure. I feel the same way." Jeremy and Kelly turned just in time to see Michael's casket disappear through the doorway. They looked at each other and silently walked away.

CHAPTER 18

Jeremy dropped Kelly off at her house to change before they took a ride. Kelly walked into her house, and the total silence unnerved her. She had never noticed feeling this way in her home. The only sound was the ticking of an old mantel clock on the fireplace. She looked around the room cautiously, as if thinking that something was wrong. Nothing looked out of place, but she felt that something was definitely wrong.

Kelly was startled by the sudden chiming of the clock as it struck the hour. Her heart was racing, and she began to smile as she realized that everything was okay. She thought about how foolish she had been to be frightened in her own home. Then a tear filled her eye as she realized what it really was that was missing. A very big part of her life was gone forever. Michael had so completely filled her life, and now she would have to move on without him. All of their plans and dreams could never be fulfilled.

Kelly walked into her bedroom and began to change her clothes. As she walked past her stereo, she turned it on. It was just too quiet in the house for her. She carefully hung up her clothes and chose a pair of faded jeans. The jeans seemed to fit her mood. As she was smoothing out the pockets she felt something prick her finger. Carefully she placed her hand in the pocket and retrieved the object. It was the football pin Michael had given her on graduation day. Gently she stroked the pin and held it to her cheek. He had told her that it didn't have to mean commitment, unless that was okay with her. She smiled at the thought of how nervous he had been that day. Some big football player he was, afraid of a little girl. She could see his face as clearly as if he were in the room. Placing the pin on her dresser, she finished getting ready.

Kelly was getting a drink of water from the refrigerator when she heard Jeremy pulling into the driveway. Hurriedly, she placed her glass in the sink, looked around to make sure everything was all right, and walked out the door.

Jeremy pulled his sports car onto the road and stared silently ahead. The breeze felt good to Kelly. It was nice not to have to worry about her hair with Jeremy. He was just a very good friend, and she could just be herself. Jeremy looked over at Kelly with more compassion in his eyes than she had ever seen before. "You okay?"

"I'm okay. Are you?"

Jeremy turned his eyes back to the road. He was silent for a moment. "I don't know what I am for sure." He looked back at Kelly. "I've never lost anyone close to me before. I lost my grandmother, but she was old, and I didn't get to see her much. But Michael, he was my best friend. More like a brother. It's going to be really weird without him."

"I know what you mean. No more phone calls. No more laughing at his dumb jokes." She looked at Jeremy and smiled. "No more watching you two trying to out-macho each other. That was pathetic."

Jeremy smiled as he thought about all of the good times he and Michael had shared together. "He sure loved to laugh, didn't he?"

Kelly smiled, lost in her own private memories of Michael. "Where would you like to go, Kelly?"

She thought for a moment. "I want to go to the river."

Jeremy thought he had heard her wrong. "Do you mean to the park?"

She looked at Jeremy and nodded. She looked straight ahead. "I want to go to the river again. I don't know why, and I may be very sorry, but I have to go." She looked at Jeremy again. "Would you mind taking me?"

Keeping his eyes fixed on the road ahead, he sighed. "No, if you want to go there, I'll take you. Are you sure that you can handle it?"

Kelly bit her lip and frowned. "No! But it's something that I feel I have to do. I know I couldn't do it alone. I'm glad you're with me."

The rest of the trip was completed in silence; Kelly and Jeremy were each lost in their own private thoughts.

Jeremy pulled his car into the parking lot, found a space, and turned off the engine. He sat there looking around the park. Everything seemed to look the same, but something felt very different. He looked at Kelly. "What now?"

Kelly looked frightened but determined. She looked at Jeremy. "I want to go down by the river." Kelly couldn't believe what she was saying. She was frightened, but just felt that it was something she needed to do. "You don't have to go with me, Jeremy. I'll understand."

Jeremy smiled. "No way! If you want to go down to the river, I'm going with you."

Kelly touched his cheek with her fingertips. "Thanks."

Jeremy helped Kelly out of the car, and the two began their walk to the site of Michael's death. Slowly and silently they walked, each one wondering how they would feel when they reached their destination. They crested the small hill that overlooked the river. Kelly stopped. Jeremy tried to watch her, making certain she was going to be alright. She stood silently, looking up and down the river.

"The water seems to be going down again. It looks so peaceful, Jeremy. How could something so lovely take someone's life?"

Kelly looked at Jeremy, hoping that somehow he could make sense of everything.

"I really don't know, Kelly. If anyone would come here right now who didn't know what had happened to Michael they would think it was just another beautiful spot. I wish I could understand it. I was really mad at God at first. Now I don't know how I feel about God." He looked at Kelly. "That's kind of scary. I never doubted Him before. Maybe I didn't really have the relationship with Him that I should have had."

"I don't really blame God. I blame myself."

Jeremy looked at Kelly in disbelief. "What in the world could you have done?"

"I don't blame myself for what happened. I blame myself for not trying harder to lead Michael to Christ. I know what Pastor Sinclair said about giving your life for someone, but what if he's wrong? What if that's not what God meant? Jeremy, Michael could be lost forever, and it would be my fault."

"Hold on, Kelly! You can't blame yourself. I could have told him, too. But it just never seemed like—"

They looked at each other and said in unison, "Like the macho thing to do."

Jeremy shook his head. "That's stupid, isn't it? But I never thought that he would be gone this soon. I guess I thought he would be around forever. Pretty dumb, huh?"

Kelly smiled. "Pretty normal, I'd say. Your macho image was at stake, and I didn't want to lose him." Kelly looked back down at the river. "I guess I lost him anyway, didn't I?"

"I guess we all did." Jeremy put his arm around Kelly's shoulder. "Come on, let's go home."

Kelly looked at Jeremy with a trace of fear in her eyes. "No! Not yet. I want to go down to the very spot that it happened. Please!"

"Are you sure, Kelly?"

"No! But I feel like I have to. I don't even understand myself. You don't have to go any farther. It's okay. I'll understand."

Jeremy shrugged his shoulders. "I may regret this, but I'll go down there with you."

Slowly, they walked to the area where Michael had given his life to save Brad's. The river had receded, and the small island that had formed was all but gone. Silently they stood before the spot. Kelly wondered what it must have been like for Michael. Had he been scared? Had he felt pain? The thought of Michael struggling on the bank of this river and then being swept downstream overwhelmed Kelly. She began to shake and tremble as tears began to flow down her face.

Jeremy reached out to Kelly. "Are you okay?"

She tried desperately to regain her composure. "I don't know, Jeremy. I can feel Michael's presence. I know it's not possible, but I can."

"Maybe we'd better go. I don't think you're ready for this yet."

Kelly snapped at Jeremy. "No! I don't know why, Jeremy, but I can't leave yet. I've got to do this."

Kelly began to walk around the spot trying desperately to piece together the scene of Michael's last moments of life. "Do you think that he knew he was dying?"

Jeremy shrugged his shoulders. "I don't know. They say that when you drown your whole life passes before you. I don't know if that's true. But he may have had time to think. I just don't know."

Jeremy joined Kelly as they walked around the small area where Michael had struggled. "Jeremy, how does God choose one person over another? Why did Michael die and Brad live?"

"You know I can't answer that! Even Pastor Sinclair couldn't answer it. I guess there's just a certain time for us to die. I don't know if we can change that. Maybe God knew all along that this would happen. I doubt that anyone knows for sure why God does certain things. He's just God, I guess."

"Can I tell you something that I'm not proud of?"

Jeremy smiled. "You know you can."

"I wish Brad had died instead of Michael. That's bad isn't it? But I really mean it."

"You can't help the way you feel any more than Michael could not help Brad. We do things before we think about the outcome sometimes. I guess that's what makes heroes—they don't really think, they just do it. Sometimes we can't help what we think either. The thoughts just come into our head. I guess what's important is what we do with those thoughts."

Jeremy stopped. "What's that?"

"Where?"

Jeremy pointed at an envelope that was stuck in the bushes beside the river. "There, in the bushes." Jeremy walked over to the envelope and picked it up. He read the front and looked at Kelly in disbelief. "Kelly! It's addressed to you."

The surprise on Kelly's face turned to curiosity. "Who's it from?"

"I don't know. There's no return address."

"Let me see it!"

Jeremy walked over and handed the letter to Kelly. She looked at Jeremy, and then began to open the letter. She read a few lines and then began to cry. "Jeremy, it's from Michael!"

"He must have dropped it when he was struggling. What does it say?"

Kelly opened the water-stained paper and began to read. "Dear Kelly, I'm not much good at saying the things I want to say. Like how much I love you." Kelly looked at Jeremy, tears filling her eyes so much that she couldn't read. She handed the letter to Jeremy.

"I know how important God is to you, even though you don't always talk about him. I see it in your eyes. In the things you say and do for people. I guess I never felt comfortable in asking a lot of questions about it. The night you took me to the Billy Graham Crusade really made an impact on me. I know I didn't say it, or act like it, but it did. I guess I didn't want to ruin my macho image." Jeremy looked at Kelly, and they both smiled.

"I thought about that night a lot. I talked to my mom about it and found out that she used to be religious. I tried to read and learn more on my own, but I guess it's time to ask for your help. A week ago I knelt down by my bed and asked God to take over my life." Jeremy began to struggle to hold back the tears and finish the letter. "I've got a lot to learn, but I think I know the right person to help get me started. I hope you don't mind this letter. I just didn't know how to just come out and say how I was feeling. All I know is that whatever the future holds for me, I'm going to trust God for what's best. I hope that's okay with you. I don't know when I'll get this letter to you, but I hope it will make you happy. I know that you've sure made me happy. I guess God is happy, too. Mr. Graham did say that all of heaven rejoices over one sinner who repents. Maybe they are rejoicing for me. I love you, Kelly Carlisle. Michael."

Jeremy finished the letter and handed it to Kelly. She was crying and laughing at the same time. "Jeremy, he is in heaven! Michael made it. I know for sure he is. This is why God brought me here today. He wanted me to find this letter. I can't believe it."

Jeremy took Kelly into his arms, and they both cried pain-relieving tears of joy. Kelly stepped back and dried her eyes. "Jeremy, I've got to go."

Jeremy looked puzzled. "What's wrong?"

Kelly smiled. "Nothing! But I have an apology to deliver. I treated Brad badly, and I think I need to go apologize. Will you take me?"

Jeremy took her hand. "You bet I will."

Hand in hand they walked up the hill away from the river's edge. When they reached the top of the hill, Kelly looked over her shoulder and whispered, "I love you, Michael."